PASSAGEWAY

Also by Gary Lee Vincent

Fiction
DARKENED HILLS
DARKENED HOLLOWS
DARKENED WATERS
DARKENED SOULS

Comic Books
THE TAILSMAN

Nonfiction
THE WINNER, THE LOSER
AGELATIONS
CONFIGURATION MANAGEMENT

Musical Releases
100 PERCENT
PASSION, PLEASURE, & PAIN
SOMEWHERE DOWN THE ROAD

Most Burning Bulb Publishing books are available at special quantity discounts for bulk purchases for sales promotions, premiums or fund raising. Special books or book excerpts can also be created to fit specific needs.

For details, write to our marketing department at info@burningbulbpublishing.com or via standard post at Burning Bulb Publishing, P.O. Box 4721, Bridgeport, WV 26431

PASSAGEWAY

GARY LEE VINCENT

Burning Bulb
PUBLISHING

Passageway
By **Gary Lee Vincent**

Burning Bulb Publishing
P.O. Box 4721
Bridgeport, WV 26330-4721
www.BurningBulbPublishing.com

Paperback ISBN: 978-0692370162

Second edition.
Printed in the United States of America.
Library of Congress Control Number: 2015900862

INTRODUCTION

Passageway represents a journey that began in 1998 and wrapped up in 2011. Of course, I didn't spend all my time over that decade writing the story, but as life typically goes, I became preoccupied with other things and my prototype fantasy story seemed to take the back burner.

It all began as a dream, or rather nightmare, that I had that centered on a ghastly scene of a Latin American farmer in a surreal world. The dream bothered me to such an extent that I thought about it for several days and decided to write it down. By itself the dream was downright disturbing, but it planted the seed for future crops to spring up.

Over the years, various ideas came to mind about how to present this alternate world of chaos and eventually a short story emerged. As each character's personality developed, the short story grew and began to take on a mind of its own.

Personally, I consider *Passageway* to be Bizarro-genre tribute to H.P. Lovecraft, intertwined with a spirit of adventure that is part *Indiana Jones,* part *Dungeons and Dragons,* and part *James Bond.* Though I should stress this is not fan fiction. *Passageway* is a very original story that takes the reader across four continents as well as to hell and back. It also conveys the inner struggle of dealing with moral pressure and how the consequences ultimately play out. It's a buckle-up ride, so get ready for some turbulence!

I also revisited this tale in late 2014 after I had some writing experience under my belt to improve on the narrative and artwork. Hopefully you will enjoy this enhanced *Second Edition* that you are now reading.

As I have alluded to, *Passageway* is a strange bird with a lot of unique angles. To keep things flowing and coherent, several people helped and I would like to acknowledge their contributions here. First, I would like to thank Carla Vincent. She was Carla Morato-Lara when I first was mining her for ideas about the Incan and Andean cultures around the year 2000.

Next, I would like to thank editorial contributors George Cunningham and Emily Walker for their insight and helping me to keep the plot on the right path when it veered from time to time. I also would like to thank horror novelist Rich Bottles Jr. for proofing this text and for listening to my banter about finishing this "never-ending" story. An appreciation goes out to renowned illustrator and fantasy artist Andy Hopp, whose wonderful drawings appear on five pages of this book.

As this is the second edition of *Passageway*, I would like to thank Sherri Hardy for copious copy editing and feedback for this edition. I also would like to thank Shatara (aka "Little Sun") for designing the awesome cover for this new edition. My sincere gratitude to all involved with this project, both past and present.

PART 1: THE PORTAL

CHAPTER 1

Our entire party was silent as we entered the crypt. This struck me as strange because I had listened to solid talk and colorful humor the entire trip. Without a doubt they were silent with excitement and expectation, for who could even guess what could be in here, with the exception of a couple of moldering corpses.

At any rate, I hoped the corpses were resting in peace and not really pissed off that we entered their tomb. I had a feeling of unrest that I tried to push to the back of my mind: Is it not one of the rules of life – you do not disturb the dead?

Of the six of us, I was the one out of place; probably because this was not my typical field of work. I am a writer, not a scientist or an archaeologist like some of the experts that were with us. It was Doug, the photographer of the group and a friend of mine, who encouraged me to go with them because there could be deeply buried, significant information that I could use in my writings. I guess he was right, for what I am about to tell you is truly powerful indeed.

About three months ago, there was an earthquake in South America. Doctor Francis (the archaeologist) had been on expedition to study a primitive culture known as the "Nachaie."

From what I was told, the existence of this tribe was not common knowledge, nor was it often discussed within the academic community. Indeed, this tribe was a virtual unknown. The study of obscure tribal cultures was something of a specialty for Doctor Francis. After extensive library and field research, Doctor was finally able to piece together a brief picture of the Nachaie culture.

The Nachaie were once part of an ancient, pre-Incan, civilization called the Tiyawanaku.

The Tiyawanaku existed over 3000 years ago and were known for their flourishing culture and vast underground ceremonial chambers.

They were originally from an area in western Bolivia, but some settled further west in Peru. To make a long story short, the earthquake exposed a portion of ground which appeared to be an entire city that had been buried for centuries.

After many days of digging, the excavation team uncovered an ancient building that contained wall inscriptions that described tribal rituals and depicted a map of the ancient city. Using this map, the research team was able to pinpoint various places of importance within the city. Most of these sites were uncovered with relative ease, but Doctor Francis was most interested in the "Tomb of the Chief" which was located in a remote area of the jungle about two miles away from the lost city.

Doctor Francis and two of his partners, scientist Fredrick Gonzalez and a digger named Ziggy discovered the exact location of this tomb about a week ago. It was then that the Doctor called my friend Doug, who had a reputation as a travel photographer and was always up for the challenge of shooting the unknown.

Doug and I were in the middle of a chess game in West Virginia when the call came. Doug was very excited and jumped at the chance to photograph a great cultural find, and I was easily talked into going along with him for the ride. Because we would be going into an uncharted tomb that, according to the Doctor, could stretch out for miles beneath the earth, *and seemed to resemble death in its truest sense,* I did protest at first. But, I had never been to South America before and I needed a vacation, so I chose to go. *Looking back now, this may have been the biggest mistake of my life.*

After a flight that took nearly eighteen hours with six connections in various South American airports, Doug and I found ourselves in Peru.

We were met at the airport by Katherine, the doctor's ever-so-stunning linguist-translator. She had a wild and sexy look to her. "Hiya boys," she said warmly. Katherine was wearing short, *very short*, brown shorts – accenting her dark tan and long, brownish-blonde hair. The shirt she was wearing hugged her in all the right places. *Wow*, I thought, *that is one hot linguist*. "Ready for a ride," she said, winking at me and smiling.

"I would take a ride with you anywhere," Doug said, grinning sheepishly and staring unapologetically at her long tan legs. I felt a twinge of jealously and wondered where that came from. As she walked away, I couldn't help but notice how nice she looked in those shorts. Doug chose that moment to elbow me in the ribs and waggle his eyebrows at me. She noticed the exchange and made a point to swing her hips a little more as she walked the rest of the way to the car. This would be an interesting trip.

From there we traveled by Jeep. It was a bumpy ride through the Peruvian highlands. After about an hour, we veered off a main road onto what looked like a narrow jungle path bordered and canopied with dense vegetation. It seemed as if the very jungle itself was closing in on us as ferns and branches brushed against the Jeep's sides, poking through the side windows and blocking out the light above us. The drive grew darker and darker until it didn't look as if there was a road at all.

Just when I thought we couldn't go any further, a dense jungle path opened into a small clearing. Katherine stopped the Jeep and announced we had arrived. I noticed the way her hair moved when she walked, then immediately chastised myself for letting her draw my attention this way. She had a similar effect on Doug as he was staring at her with his mouth open and a dumb look on his face.

I felt that stab of jealousy again. Katherine turned around, "We really are going to have to light a fire under you slack asses. You have to get a move on; there will be plenty of time to look around later." There was that sexy wink again. Time to focus on work; I was anxious to get to our destination.

We walked about a short ways and met up with Doctor Francis and his crew. I could tell that this forested area had been recently cleared. They had set up a tent in what appeared to be the center of town in the lost city.

To me it looked as if a large meteor had struck the earth and exposed a deep crater. The earthquake had literally blasted through the side of a mountain and huge chunks of rock lay scattered about. It appeared that Doctor Francis and his staff had been working for several weeks excavating, as various areas around the crater where exposed.

I remember Ziggy making references to "Old Peak." I later came to find that he was talking about Machu Picchu, an ancient Incan city located on the mountain ridge above the Urubamba Valley. Doctor Francis told me that we were actually closer to Espiritu Pampa, or "Vilcabamba," as it has also been called.

Vilcabamba was burned to the ground during the fall of the Incan Empire, I remembered reading in a history book somewhere.

We exchanged introductions, the friendliest of which was with Yurak, a white mixed-breed dog whom the camp adopted as their mascot. At first sight, I thought that a wolf might have wandered into the camp. Yurak wasn't really big, but he just had that wolf-like look about him. He was muscular and thin with a long nose and blue eyes. He looked like he could be a cross between a Siberian husky and a German shepherd, only a bit smaller than either breed. *Maybe you're part coyote, boy,* I thought to myself as he approached.

Yurak greeted me as if he had known me all his life. As his tail wagged excitedly, I felt there was something special about this dog. Ziggy said he just showed up at the camp one day and had been around ever since. "No one came to claim him and he doesn't give anybody any trouble, so we just let him stick around," he said with a grin.

Some of the Doctor's staff stayed back at the main dig site in the uncovered city to continue their archeological work. One of the girls, Sylvia, had prepared several backpacks for us to take on our journey. Sylvia was an olive-skinned Bolivian who was very helpful to Doctor Francis' team. I was told that she was the camp's cook. She would be staying behind to prepare the meals for the crew, including ourselves, once we returned from our expedition.

Sylvia handed me my pack. I looked in the backpack and noticed two flashlights, a one-liter bottle of water, some paper towels, and four bread-like pastries that I later learned were empanadas. "Gracias," I said as we left.

Though it was purely coincidental, everyone on the "away" team except me was wearing either light brown or tan-colored clothes. I, on the other hand, was wearing blue jeans and a black T-shirt, which added to my feeling of being an outsider. I caught myself looking at Katherine's ass, just for a moment, and found that she, too, was wearing brown.

Well, at least I *thought* it was a moment. "Are you enjoying the view," she startled me back to reality and I realized I must have been staring longer than I thought. I was speechless, and embarrassed that she caught me. "Next time take a picture, it will last a lot longer." She smiled and sauntered off leaving me there blushing furiously.

The entire walk through the dense, mosquito-infested jungle was lively with humor and fellowship as the group chattered like children right before Christmas. I wondered if they all might be taking this entire expedition too lightly. My feeling of impending doom did not seem to be resonating with the rest of the group. I began to think I was overreacting to the whole situation. My gut was usually right so I would still proceed with caution.

My gaze kept traveling back to Katherine, the way she carried herself with ease while keeping up with the conversation was alluring. I almost walked right into a tree and had to remind myself to pay attention. I needed better focus, or the whole walk would be one accident after another. That was all I needed: to end up breaking something before we even got to the crypt!

Katherine would be right to go after Doug then. This thought disturbed me as I narrowly missed stepping into a small creek that was running by our path.

"You with us today?" Doug called out. "You are acting drunk." I just ignored his comments and kept walking. *Get it together man*, I said to myself, *she is just a girl and your work is way more important. Besides, you are getting WAY ahead of yourself. You don't even know if she likes you!*

Yurak followed us for a little while then turned and headed back to the camp. We were at the edge of a large river. "Curious dog," Fredrick observed. "He never goes any further than here then turns around."

Interesting observation, I thought to myself. *He must have the same feeling about the tomb as I do.*

We walked along the river's edge as the terrain rose steadily upwards. Close to the entrance of the tomb, we came across a small village. There were several huts and dark-skinned, native children were playing near them. A couple of the native adults looked up as we walked by but they said nothing.

We climbed even further and stopped to rest near a house, or what could be passed off as a house. The "house" was a run-down shack that Ziggy said belonged to a farmer named Pabilito. It was built with oak and had a thatched roof. It reminded me of a cross between a turn-of-the-century cabin and a hay barn that I had seen back in the States, but I did not share this with the others.

The house had a large porch with wood railings and an outside staircase ascending on the right. There were open rafters supporting the sagging roof and the place looked like it had seen better days.

"The farmer," Ziggy said, "has six kids. He keeps them working from dusk till dawn every day in his garden 'round back." I looked at the area he was referring to and noticed a skinny woman wearing a bandanna on her head and swinging a sickle. She appeared to be cleaning up weeds.

9

"That's Mobbi," Ziggy continued, "Short for Modabida. She's his wife. That whole bunch – *always* working! He's a slave driving son-of-a-bitch!"

As if on cue, Pabilito came out on the porch. He was a stern, weathered man, contrary to his colorful red poncho. Looking down, he saw us and waved. We waved back. *Hard work is a way of life for these people,* I thought. I saw he had a large rolled rope in his hands. *Probably getting ready to fix something,* I presumed.

We continued up the embankment and approached what seemed to be a large hole dug into the hillside. A the back of the hole, a manmade wall and a sealed door could be seen outlined in the dirt. From the grins surrounding me, I knew we had arrived.

"So that is the crypt," I said, sounding so much calmer than I felt. The nagging feeling in my stomach was getting worse. Why did I choose this? Wasn't I excited? I love adventure, or at least I thought I did. I wished I was still in my office at home, writing about things that did not involve gallivanting in the unknown.

"Aye," replied Doctor Francis, "The time has come for us to venture into the bowels of the earth. I am sure that you will have plenty to write about when we are finished."

"I'm sure I will," I said with a grin. The truth was, we had just entered a gaping hole in the earth and I was already uneasy. They say you should go with your gut in situations like this. Had I gone with my gut I would have avoided a lot of trouble.

With Katherine watching I couldn't be a total wimp, so I sucked it up and prepared for the descent. I watched her in front of me as she eagerly prepared along with everyone else. I felt respect for this woman I had just met; I guess this is why I wanted to impress her with my bravery.

There was a large tree that had been growing over the entrance prior to the earthquake. With its long root structure growing downwards and over the ground, along with its moss-covered bark, I could see why the entrance had been overlooked. It was perfectly camouflaged in the flora and fauna of the forest.

Now they do. The earthquake did a real number on the overturned tree. Ripping it from the ground, the earthquake pulled the tree outwards at a profanely backward angle and revealed the gaping hole.

Looking inward about ten feet we could see a large stone that looked very heavy. It was not natural, though. It didn't quite look like a rock, but rather a dry, polished square, stone slab; flush to the earth and surrounded by dirt where the tree's roots had once been. I remember reaching out to touch it – it was cool like the granite surface of a monument you would find in a typical cemetery.

"Cemetery," why did I have to think that? Snap out of it, I thought, *you are in control here.*

Ziggy had used a crowbar to open the sealed entrance, which seemed unresponsive and formidable, given the way he was struggling. My inner thoughts were racing: *The tomb should have stayed sealed. Something's down there and you know it.* Every part of my being was telling me to run the other way, and to stop this mad trip into the Earth. Why in the world was I still moving forward? Was it some kind of morbid interest in the unknown? Was I looking forward to the danger that surely awaited us at the bottom of the tomb?

Part of me probably thought I could save Katherine from some sort of danger and be her hero. This was a ridiculous fantasy, of course, because I had first laid eyes on this woman only a few hours before. Why did I care if she thought favorably of me? Sure she was very attractive and undoubtedly a cunning linguist as she was the team's translator. I grinned to myself. Throw bravery onto her list of many attributes and I suppose that was enough for me to risk my neck to protect her. Perhaps this is why I was sticking around, even though I could feel something bad was coming.

Once I climbed past the seal, a cool air could be felt as the temperature changed from the hot, muggy outside to the subterranean climate below.

To be honest, I expected to see nests of poisonous snakes scattered about the floor and along the walls of the tomb's foyer, but there were none. There did appear to be a large amount of dust which had collected on the ground and the darkness was blinding after being in the bright sunlight for so long.

As I mentioned before, the entire party was silent as we began our venture into the crypt. Doctor Francis was a relatively tall man and he had to bend down because of the low ceiling. I wondered how long he could keep exploring in that uncomfortable position.

It did not help that Katherine was right behind him, and was bent over as well. I could see her perfectly round bottom every time someone's flashlight passed her way. I tried very hard to focus on anything else. I really had to start seeing her as a colleague and not someone to gawk at like a lovesick teenager. She made me feel inadequate for some reason. This was not a feeling I was used to, or happy about.

The entry room was not a room at all but rather a narrow, dark corridor descending downward. The Doctor pointed out that he believed this corridor to be the entry vein to a large network of catacombs below the earth's surface. All I could think of was how many dead bodies the catacombs contained. I started to feel like I was being watched. The feeling made the hair on the back of my neck stick up, and I actually rubbed my neck to try to make it stop. Doug looked at me strangely, but he did not say anything.

I wondered how long it would take for our group to get lost since none of us really knew our way around. *Hell, even the doctor doesn't know for sure – I watched them break the seal of the tomb!*

Don't be such a pessimist! cried my inner voice, *Just think of what you are about to discover...*

CHAPTER 2

Each member of our party was required to carry two sources of light – one for now and one for later in case the primary light would happen to fail. Thinking of Sylvia, I reached into my backpack and pulled out my flashlight number one. *An empanada might be good about now,* I thought as my hand brushed against one. Doug brought out gadgets for his camera equipment and between all of us there was plenty of light to see by.

The walls of this passageway appeared smooth and chiseled. There was a damp, old smell throughout – it was the smell of centuries long ago, of times long forgotten; it was the musty smell of something better left alone. It was the smell of *something* . . . something evil? Maybe. It was the smell . . . *the smell of death.*

About fifty yards down the slowly descending corridor, there was a sudden turn. It appeared to be a 90 degree turn and the wall we faced at the turn was plastered with what I thought were hieroglyphics.

"Yes!" Doctor Francis proclaimed. "Fredrick, come quick! What do you make of these?"

Fredrick was traveling in the middle of our group. Katherine had told me along the way that Fredrick Gonzalez had a reputation as one of the best interpreters of pictorial language. I noticed that Doug was already getting his camera out as the scientist thumbed through his notes.

"Gentleman and lady," Fredrick said winking as he turned to Katherine, "history is about to be rewritten today!"

"Amazing," concurred Doctor Francis.

"It truly is," Fredrick replied. "It has been thought for centuries that pre-Incan civilization did not have a written language. These geoglyphs prove that theory to be incorrect," he said with a smile.

"Now, let's see what it says!" He pulled out a tiny notebook from his backpack and began to go over some notes he had made from prior explorations. He studied the wall for a while, jotting down some additional information in his book, then spoke.

"Though I cannot say with one hundred percent certainty, I believe they called this *The Passageway of Souls – The Gateway of the Sun.*" He held his arms wide open as he said this to express both the pictures we were looking at and the chamber we were standing in.

He turned back to the wall. The symbols seemed to illustrate a row of people lying horizontally, as opposed to standing upright, to the left of a giant arch. "The arch," he said, "represents a passageway. These," he said pointing to the line of vertically-lying people, "are the dead."

To the right of the arch, there were skeletons that were standing upright and walking toward a round image of a puma. He studied it further. "The puma could be the sun and," he stopped and then raised his voice with excitement. "I get it! I think it says, *'Only the dead may travel here on their journey to the underworld.'*"

I felt truly uneasy as he said this. I looked over at Katherine who simply shrugged and gave a slight, unsteady smile. "You're not afraid of some long-dead Boogie Man are ya, tough guy?" She said, unable to hide a tremble in her voice.

I was beginning to feel prickles on the back of my neck, and I fought the urge to rub it again. Anything that says "only the dead travel here" makes me very nervous. For that matter, anything that mentions the underworld probably would not lead to anything good. I thought again how easy it would be to turn around and leave. I turned around to look at the route we had traveled down, and ran right into Katherine.

"Oh goodness, you scared me half to death!" she said. I was standing only inches from her. I could smell her shampoo. She was looking me in the eyes, and her breathing was heavy from being startled.

I thought that she was blushing, and she seemed a little flustered as she said, "I'm going to back away now."

Fredrick and Doctor Francis spent about twenty-five minutes examining the wall of symbols. We all had adequate time to absorb and mull over the warning.

I joined Fredrick and the doctor at the wall. The next image I saw was a warrior-like skeleton holding what appeared to be a spear or pole-arm in his hand looking down in the direction of the cave.

Though I have had no formal training in the study of geoglyphic art, this image troubled me. *Warriors of undead realms guard that which is sacred.*

He did not look like someone I would want to tangle with in this dark cave. My imaginings of mummies and snakes seemed tame compared to this guy.

"The Tomb of the Chief must be this way," announced the doctor. Ziggy led the way as we pushed on.

It was just as the warning faded from our lights that I felt a *change*. It was unsettling. I could not put my finger

17

on it, but *something happened.* Was it the temperature? Was it my imagination? *No, "Only the dead shall pass!"*

The warning was turning over and over in my head and just then, I looked around. The group all looked solemn and emotionless. *They feel it too. They KNOW something's wrong.*

We traveled about 100 yards or so further down the passageway. It was then that the chiseled look of the corridor took on the appearance of a cavern. The temperature seemed to drop, confirming my ideas that we were truly underground now. Before, we were probably in a manmade antechamber of some sort, but now we were in a natural passageway.

My thoughts were confirmed by tiny droplets of water that were striking my head from above, probably from a water source close by. In fact, I could hear a faint trickle from somewhere further down the cave.

"This is amazing!" exclaimed Dr. Francis. "It is as if the Nachaie discovered this cavern and built their ceremonial chamber above it. They linked their catacombs via the tunnel we just traveled through!"

"It's kinda chilly down here," Katherine said, shivering a little.

I took notice once again at the way she was dressed. If we were outside, this outfit would be perfectly normal (*except for the extreme shortness of her shorts*), but in the cave, it truly was downright cold. Just barely, I could see gooseflesh on her arms and muscular legs.

Up ahead, we could see that the passageway was opening up into a larger room. Our lanterns could make out the silhouette of a corpse lying at its entrance. We quickened our pace.

The body was that of a Conquistador. It was covered with dust and the man was cloaked in rusted armor, wearing a helmet that was once ordained with feathers. The feathers now looked like sticks with cobwebs and the man's face was nothing more than a skull.

He appeared to have died while leaning up against the cavern wall. Knee-high boots adorned his skeletal feet and his sword was at his side. In his hand, he held a book.

"What an amazing find," Doctor Francis said. He reached down and carefully picked up the book. It was very old and he studied it for what seemed like a long time. Finally, he looked up, "It's a diary and it's written in Spanish!"

He carefully turned the brittle, almost crumbling pages to the last entry...

30 September 1530

I, Philippe Pazarro hereby make my last account. May God have mercy on the soul of he who finds this journal.

I have spent days tracking the remnant of Capac's army. We made a final stand at their Skull Fortress deep in the mountains. I saw the glistening light of the setting sun for the last time as it reflected off the face of the Fort's entrance.

I followed their captain into its mouth thinking it was just a single room, but like Jonah in the belly of the giant fish, it has swallowed me.

It is as if I have seen Satan himself and the Armies of Hell – a force that no man can reckon.

I have made it back, across the Lake of Fire, across the Plains of Death. I alone have escaped the wolf. Alas, I am a fool – there is no escape!

PASSAGEWAY

The earthquake has blocked my way and there is no retreat. Blessed be the outside world.

My only consolation as I end my days and this diary is that perhaps the Beast of Hell and his minions are also trapped. Perhaps that is the Lord's will and if so, may this tomb stay sealed for a thousand years.

I cannot continue. That which was started in the spirit cannot be completed in the flesh. To the cross and the blood of Jesus Christ I cling. May no man know what I have seen.

The beast is real. It devours all. It cannot be stopped! I have seen his auburn eyes with my own and may I never see them again.

CHAPTER 3

Francis handed the book to Katherine, who placed it carefully in preserving plastic and then in her backpack. As we walked around the conquistador we came to what I perceived as a major obstacle.

We entered into a vast room of the cavern. The passageway seemed to end and our forward progress was blocked by water. It appeared to be a large lake, or possibly an underground river. I did notice however, that the water was not clear but rather thick, brown, and murky. Other than swimming, I could not visibly see another way around. *Looks like we came all this way for nothing.*

I could only imagine what horrors were underneath that water, what death and decay lay on its floor. I shuddered at the thought.

Ziggy walked over to the edge of the water and sat his primary lantern down at an angle that illuminated a large portion of the room where we were standing. I saw a wondrous spectacle of natural formations. There were wet stalagmites and stalactites throughout this room. They took on a white, frosty appearance from the minerals which formed them.

My momentary wondering was jolted slightly when I observed motion on the damp, slick wall of the cave near where Ziggy was standing. His light flickered, making reflections that looked like ghostly shadows moving in an eerie way across the cave's walls. *Like demons dancing.*

I was about to ask what we were going to do about the water blockade when Fredrick Gonzalez spoke up. "Look!" he said as he pointed across the room. "See the steam. Be careful – this water is boiling!"

Gonzalez was right. The water *was* boiling. Despite the coolness of the cave, we all took notice of the fact that there was a great source of heat emitting from the murky water below.

"Geothermal activity," announced Doctor Francis. "I didn't expect this. It seems that the earthquake must have cracked a plate in the cavern's floor causing a mixture of sulfur and lava just under where we are standing."

Great, I thought, *we're right on top of an active volcano!*

"We will need some more equipment." Dr. Francis continued. "I think it would be best for us to return to the surface and head back to base camp. We can return tomorrow once we have some more gear."

"I'd like to get a sampling kit down here and see what's in this water," Gonzalez said.

"Let me get a few shots first!" Doug proposed. He eagerly whipped his camera out and started shooting. The flash filled the room with a blinding white light and for several minutes I simply could not see to continue.

"Aggh!" yelled Gonzalez. He was looking directly at the flash bulb when Doug snapped the shot. Ziggy laughed, but I could not even see him, as my startled eyes were still recovering.

"Damn, Doug!" I said. "What kind of flash are you using?"

"It's the most powerful flash in the world, of course! It might seem bright, but these pictures will come out perfectly. It will be like we were shooting this cave in the daylight!"

I felt no point in arguing but wondered why the flash never affected me when he photographed the geoglyphs earlier in the passageway. Just then, I heard Katherine scream.

"There's a hand! I saw a hand!"

The crowd looked around to see what startled her, but we just couldn't see the cause of her anguish. *We are all probably blind from Doug's flash.*

"Oh no! Look at the water!" Katherine continued. "Just look at the water!"

As my vision marginally came back I could almost see what she was talking about. It appeared as if there was something in the middle of the water. It was so dark that none of us could really tell *what* it was, but *something* was out there. The bubbling water just bobbed it around in the shadows of the cave.

"Doug, I *saw* it when you took the picture!" Katherine frantically exclaimed.

"She's right!" Ziggy revealed. "Look at the bodies!" The entire group was looking at an area in the back right portion of the room where Ziggy was pointing.

"Sweet Jesus!" exclaimed Dr. Francis. "The water must have flooded the burial chamber!"

I still could not see well enough to make out the details that the others were seeing, but I was not sure that I wanted to. *I just want to get the hell out of here!*

The group was rumbling and moving around and I tried to see what they were seeing. I squinted toward the water's edge near where I was standing and I let my eyes adjust. Almost as if I *knew* what was coming, I knelt down for a closer look.

From the murky depths of the internecine water came an exposed stump of a neck barely hanging on to a decayed, rotten head. The corpse had been mostly decapitated and it swiveled with the current. It turned around and *looked* at me. My eyes were no doubt in perfect focus as I stared into the deep and pitted sockets where its eyes once were. The flesh remaining around the head was pitted, blue, and dirty. Gaping flesh-holes exposed the skull. There was no nose and its teeth were haphazardly lodged in an opened mouth, as if it were screaming in ageless terror.

"Horse shit!" I yelled and stumbled back. I bumped into Gonzalez, but he grabbed me, stopping me from falling.

Just then, the ground beneath us began to shake violently and it was as if the cave itself let out a moan.

As it shook, the water trembled and I could not help but shine the light towards it. How I wish I wouldn't have. I was greeted by three bodies lying together and as the water trembled, each one of them stared through me. Was it possible for the dead to stare? I wish there were ways to erase memories. Not even close to the most horrific thing I saw on this trip, those black skeletal stares will haunt me for the rest of my life.

Then at once, the vibrations stopped.

"Another earthquake," Katherine yelled. "We better get out of here!"

"Okay guys, listen," Dr. Francis announced. "We need to get back to the camp; check out the seismic activity from above ground and when it's safe, we'll come back here with a full crew!" He turned to Doug, "I think you will have more pictures to take than what you had expected." He paused, "Let's go!"

We all started back up the passageway, making our way around the fallen Spanish soldier, and we walked for over twenty minutes before we came back to the manmade portion of the corridor. I took notice of the fact that we were all walking briskly, but despite this, it seemed to take *so long* just to get here, which was midway in our assent. *You're just paranoid – Remember you're walking uphill – It takes longer.*

"We must have walked a long way," I said to no one in particular.

Much to my surprise it was Dr. Francis who answered me. "It seems we *have* been walking for a while" He shook his head, "Maybe it's just our imagination. That was some nasty shit back there!"

"Doctor," I asked, "why did the head in the water still have flesh? I'd think something that old would have just been a skull."

"Many of the dead were mummified," he replied. "A few years ago in Puruchuco, thousands of Incan mummies – many with hair, skin, and eyes intact – were excavated from a large Incan graveyard. They were in cocoons. They found entire families wrapped together in layers of cotton and intricate textiles."

"You said thousands?" I asked.

"Yes, over 10,000." He replied.

"Tupac Amaru," Katherine interjected. "It was a shanty town named after the last Incan ruler. Back in the 1980s, guerrilla activity forced thousands of Peruvian refugees to find shelter in the somewhat stable Lima. Many sought to build shelter on Purchuco, the Incan cemetery. They called the place Tupac Amaru.

"They built these makeshift houses right over the dead." She paused, and then continued, "But they are

25

afraid of the dead because of daña – "the illness" – which they believe the dead bring when they live over them."

"Tupac Amaru, the man, was executed by Spanish conquerors in 1572." Katherine finally concluded.

"Look, not much further now." It was Ziggy, obviously wanting to change subjects. He was pointing to the bend in the passage where we all had looked at the geoglyphs. Though I felt a sense of familiarity, I could not help but continue to feel uneasy. *Something was just not right.*

I made it a point to walk next to the wall where we had observed the symbols. They were not there.

"Frederick, come over here," I said. He quickly noticed the same thing I did.

"Very odd. Where the hell did they go?!" Frederick Gonzalez exclaimed. "Where are the geoglyphs?!"

Dr. Francis was concerned, to say the least, but he maintained his professionalism nevertheless. "I know that we did not take a wrong turn anywhere – for there was only one way down. There can only be one way up." Shrugging his shoulders in a way that I perceived as trying to convince himself that this was making sense he added, "I'm sure we will see them tomorrow when we get our bearings straight."

"Yeah," Katherine added, "let's just get out of here!" She was obviously spooked. I was about to add *"You're not afraid of the Boogie Man are ya, chiquitita?"* but I thought better of it.

When turning the corner that led us onto a direct course to the entrance, I felt a strong rush of warm air hit my face. *The Peruvian outdoors,* I thought, *how nice to see you again.*

We made it to the seal of the tomb and then I realized that my fears *did* have justification. The outside was not the same as we had left it.

Even while letting my eyes adjust to the light from the outdoors, I knew that we had gone from bad to worse. It was if we had just stepped into hell.

The sky was deep lavender gray, dark, and threatening. White cumulus clouds hung low, shooting powerful bolts of lightning across the horizon. I heard the wind *(or least I thought it was the wind)* howl, but I did not feel a breeze. And though I stood with five others beside me, I felt alone.

The ground was not plush and green like we had left it, but rather scorched and charred. Sand, instead of foliage, covered the ground and it was dirty brown. The earth appeared to have been incinerated. There were no trees, no weeds, no grass, no vegetation whatsoever. I did not see any signs of what I had encountered before. There appeared to be no *life.*

At first I thought that maybe a volcano had erupted and scorched the ground, but truly didn't know what to think. It was then that I saw the old farmer's house still standing down below our path.

"Come," said Dr. Francis. That was all he said as he began to walk toward the house. That was all that anyone could have said.

I don't know what made me do it, but I looked back just as we started off the hill. There was no big, overgrown and broken tree. No roots and no foliage around the entrance. What once was a hole dug in the hill by Dr. Francis and his staff was now a gaping rock entrance – a gaping rock entrance in the shape of a skull.

"Doug, you may want to photograph that," I said with a lump in my throat as I pointed to the skull.

PASSAGEWAY

"Oh my..." Doug said as his thoughts trailed off. He fumbled nervously for the camera and I thought for a moment that this sure and steady photographer might actually drop his camera. He did not.

CHAPTER 4

The wind blew hot, arid, and stale against our skin. Though the humidity was gone from the once lush jungle, it somehow seemed much hotter than before. I looked at the others and despite my beliefs I refrained from telling them that we were in hell. They sensed it and I think they *knew* it, and shortly our worst fears were confirmed.

"Come," Dr. Francis announced. "Let's see if we can find the farmer." Despite the inexplicably altered environment, it *did* appear as if we could make out the outline of the farmer's house down the slope below us.

The house was there. It was *not* the same. The old wood trim had turned to faded gray and had started to rot. The roof was sagging and the thatching appeared disheveled, much of it on the ground scattered around the house's perimeter.

The river in front of the house was still there, but it was almost dry. What once was a soaking, flowing vein of water was now a barren creek bed. Only a trickle of water flowed, but it didn't look like water. It was orange and sulfuric.

Something that struck me as strange was a heavy, patchy fog that hung over the ground. Our party seemed to be trying to avoid it like it was radiating danger. It was an eerie mist and I got the sense that it was actually breathing. We had to walk through it, and everyone hesitated and looked at each other not knowing what to expect. After a minute everyone took a step forward and collectively gasped. The fog was cold, and, despite the hot temperature around me, it chilled me to the bone. I felt like the fog was inside of me making me angry and sad at the same time. The mist seemed to grasp forcefully for my soul. I had never felt such sorrow in my life. The cold seemed unending, and I thought I would be trapped in this horrible cold existence forever. When we finally trudged into a clear place all the bad feelings dissipated. I didn't feel at peace, by any means, but I wasn't cold, angry, and incredibly depressed anymore.

"Let's try to avoid the death fog from now on," I said in a detached voice I did not recognize. Everyone nodded in agreement and we moved forward, walking all the way around the patchy fog and going to great lengths to avoid it.

Being from West Virginia, I had seen a lot of coal mines. Coal contains sulfur, and sometimes a bi-product of mining is the sulfuric acid run-off when the coal is exposed to the surface air. Although I have seen my share of this in coal country, I was pretty confident that there were no such mines close by, and wasn't this a wetland just hours ago?

As I pondered this geological quandary, nothing could prepare us for the wretched horror awaiting us as we came around the house. Hanging from one of the porch rafters was the farmer, Pabilito, his decaying corpse sun-blistered and blackened. One eye was missing, as if plucked by a vulture.

"My God!" Ziggy exclaimed.

"What happened? What the hell's going on?" Dr. Francis added.

The wind suddenly picked up again and carried horribly rancid smells our way. Katherine gagged and I quickly turned away. We all proceeded toward the rear of the house to get our bearings when we came across an even more ghastly sight.

31

Impaled on a fence post in the rear yard of the property was Mobbi, Pabilito's wife. *Modabida, Ziggy had called her.* On a face of sheer terror with her head arched back, her eyes were open looking up blankly at the ever-so-menacing sky. Her mouth had age-old blood spittle oozing from one side and it had dried around her cheeks and neck.

The fence post was not like a traditional rounded post, but pointed, like a sharp spear, and was protruding through Mobbi's chest. I am not sure what disturbed me most, seeing her impaled or seeing the sickle still in her clenched fist.

For a moment, I watched as the entire scene played out in my mind's eye...

***

Work you bitch! I could almost hear Pabilito scream at her.

But I cannot, please, she replied.

Where's Diego? Where're the others?

They are gone, they will never work for you again! She screamed.

What did you do to them? He demanded

She laughed an insane and uncanny laugh. A laugh so loud, so ghastly, it echoed through the valley with its dark overtones. She shrugged her shoulders.

Damn it, you tell me now!

She raised the sickle, dripping in fresh blood.

No! He screamed. Pabilito ran around the back. The children were gone.

What did you do? They started to fight in the back yard.

She lunged at him, bringing the sickle down violently. She missed.

Pabilito kicked her back and she fell to the dirt.

He darted to the edge of the property, back turned momentarily.

She was right behind him. With fury, she lunged again. Pabilito spun around, angling the pointy fence post at her and simultaneously yanking it from the ground

You're going to pay for this, Pabilito yelled.

Mobbi lunged again, this time striking Pabilito across the chest with the sickle. She drew blood and howled with the manical laughter of the insane.

Pabilito hit her with the fence post. She fumbled backward and lost her bearings. Pabilito ran forward with all his might and jabbed the spear/post through the center of her back and out through her chest.

She screamed with horror and collapsed impaled upon the post.

Blood splattered all over the ground and up onto Pabilito's chest. Mobbi's blood mixed with the blood on his chest formed the creepiest union of man and wife I have ever imagined.

Almost in a trance, Pabilito lifted the post with Mobbi on it and returned it to the original hole in the ground from which it came. He was bleeding badly.

The rope that I saw him with just hours before had been on the porch. Pabilito ascended the stairs, made a noose with the rope and hanged himself.

I watched as he swayed in the breeze...

He did not even struggle; he had this look on his face like a man who lost everything. As he took his last breath his eyes froze in that sad state.

***

About that time Katherine touched my hand, she looked worried. "Don't stare at her," she whispered. "There's nothing we can do."

I shook my head. *How long had I been staring?* I thought.

Before I knew it, Doug had pulled out his camera and began taking pictures of the ghastly scene. As he was zooming in to photograph Mobbi, I noticed the rust colored stains on the sickle. *Blood,* I thought, *but whose?*

Just then, Doctor Francis pointed out a wash basin in the back yard. "Look, over there!"

We all looked over in morbid curiosity. A small hand lay over the side, sticking out from within the tub. My heart was sickened and I did not want to go over there.

The basin was full of coagulated blood. Sticking out of it on the edge was a severed arm and hand. *It's her kids,* my mind raced, *she cut them up with a sickle and they're in the basin!*

"Guys, what are we going to do?" I asked.

"We need to get back to the camp," Doctor Francis replied. "We need to figure out what happened here; and what is happening out there!" He threw up his hands in protest. "Right now, I do not have an explanation."

Ziggy muttered something in Quechua and shook his head. We looked at each other uneasily and the group began to walk in the general direction of the camp.

CHAPTER 5

In hell there is no night, only twilight. Its dark, lavender sky does not change. The storms are always approaching, but the rain never comes to quench the thirsty land, dampen the air, or lower the heat. Pray if you dare, but don't expect an answer.

The walk to the camp in the raging heat was unbearable. I could never in my life remember being so thirsty, so dry. I reached into my backpack and took out the liter of water that Sylvia had been so kind to pack. It was warm, but refreshing.

I almost thought of walking through a patch of mist to cool off for a minute, but it terrified me, and I decided the heat was more bearable than the cold feeling of death.

Throughout the walk, images of what I had just witnessed kept playing over and over in my mind. All were quiet as we walked.

Everyone was stunned by what we had seen, and each kept their own thoughts, trying to come to grips with the shift in reality, that only an hour before had been ordered and understood. Now everything was changed, and I felt nothing but foreboding as we neared our camp.

I pictured the dismembered children; I pictured their faces while they watched their mother hack them and their siblings to pieces. I wished I did not have such a vivid imagination. It was my imagination wasn't it? I could not see what actually happened could I? I pushed that thought out of my head.

We crested a hill that overlooked the camp. The valley was desolate. The campsite looked like it had been hit by a long forgotten tornado. Equipment was scattered everywhere. There were no signs of life, no Sylvia, and no crew. We slowly made our way down the hill in utter disbelief.

The Jeep that Katherine picked us up in was overturned. The front passenger wheel was missing – well, not really – it appeared to have landed a few meters from the vehicle; flat and dirty.

She walked to the other side of it, and let out a terrified scream. I rushed to her side to see what was wrong. Standing there, as if ready to attack, was a large dog baring every tooth in its mouth. It looked like a mix of many breeds and was very muscular. I thought it looked like it had some wolf blood. It was very still; I thought it was just waiting to attack. As I continued to stare I realized it was not moving. In fact, it was not even blinking.

"Holy shit," I said. "It's dead."

"What do you mean?" Katherine said, clearly knowing what I meant.

"Look at him, he looks like he was scared," I replied, as I walked closer to him.

I put my arm around her in an attempt to comfort her, but as she buried her head in my shoulder I felt slightly inappropriate. She regained her composure and I looked back at the dog. He did look scared.

His lips were pulled all the way back in a menacing growl, but his eyes were wide with fear. Whatever killed him where he stood froze him perfectly. I got the feeling he was scared to death, and nothing had even touched him. To say that this unnerved me is an understatement. Everyone else looked terrified, but no one said anything. What could

37

they say!? The dog was one of the few once-living things we had laid eyes upon, and he had met a fate worse than the family at the farm house. I should have known by the rotten smell radiating from the carcass that it was a dead dog. My brain just took a minute to register that the smell was coming from the dog, because it appeared to still be alive. *This place is getting stranger and more sinister by the minute*, I thought.

Papers were strewn across ground. I dared not pick any up, for I dreaded what the pages might say. *"Only the dead may travel here on their journey to the underworld,"* I heard Fredrick's voice echo in my head.

"I think we have entered into a dimension of evil," Katherine said solemnly. "Something happened in the passageway."

"I agree," I said. "Toto, I don't think we're in Kansas anymore." I suppose I had secretly hoped to arouse a smile from the ever-so-gorgeous assistant, but my attempts at humor failed in light of the situation.

"Thanks for trying," she said, "I do not feel like smiling at the moment."

"Francis, please tell us what you know about the area we are in," I asked.

"Vilcabamba la Vieja was a lost city and the last refuge of the Incas. We are near it. After the Incan empire fell, the city was burned and the area became part of the Peruvian backwaters. The location of Vilcabamba was forgotten.

"Many years later, in 1892, three Cuzqueños – natives of the city Cuzco – visited the remote area..." Francis paused as if struggling to remember something.

"There was a journal that one of them kept that described what they found. It was written in Quechan. No one has ever seen the journal, but it has been rumored that some of the Incas found a way to another city where they escaped from the Spanish."

"Was it Machu Picchu?" I inquired.

"No," Francis replied. "Some thought this to be the case. However, it was postulated in the journal that it was the Nachaie that helped a large number of Incans escape the Spanish onslaught. They fled to Ukhu Pacha Tiwanaku."

"Ukhu Pacha is Quechan for 'hell.'" Katherine said, somewhat surprised that she was just learning about this little detail in the journal.

"Yes," Doctor Francis affirmed. "Although I should point out that, according to my interpretation of the legend, hell was just a description of the long foot journey through the Peruvian Andes over to their ancient city of Tiwanaku in western Bolivia.

"But, perhaps I was mistaken," Francis lamented in a voice that was almost a whisper.

"Tell me about Tiwanaku," I said, "because I'm not familiar with any of this and it would be good to know, given our predicament."

"Around 1500 BC, Tiwanaku was a small farming village. Over the centuries that followed, it grew significantly. People were making pilgrimages there because of certain..." he paused, "religious reasons."

"What kind of religious reasons?" I asked.

"Tiwanaku was a cult city/state," he replied. "The city's elite kept many secrets inside its walls. There was one building they called Akipana."

He gulped, "At Akipana, people were disembodied – ripped from limb to limb – and left to lay out for all to see. It is speculated that this ritual was a form of dedication to their gods." *Looks like Mobbi had a little Akipana action going out back at the hut,* I thought to myself.

"In the Bolivian archeological site of Tiwanaku, there was also a "Gateway to the Sun." I've been there, however, that one, is more weather-centered."

Fredrick added: "I have been there too. That gateway has twelve faces representing twelve months. They are positioned above thirty kneeling subjects. Here is a picture," he showed a small newspaper clipping that someone had drawn. He had taped it to a page in the notebook he was referencing.

I asked, "It would appear as if there were a lot of these archways in the ancient world. Could it be that they weren't merely symbolic, but rather a passageway into someplace else, say intra-dimensionally?"

"I cannot say." Francis added. "But if so, we are in a place where myth and history collide."

"Wait one minute," Doug interjected. "You're telling me that Ukhu Pacha Tiwanaku is not in our *world?* Am I hearing you right?"

"More like an alter-world," Francis replied. "The journal was a Necronomicon – a book of the dead -- containing many strange accounts of ghosts and devils, in lands similar to ours, yet different and macabre."

"Have you read this journal?" Katherine asked.

"I have not," Francis replied. "In fact, no one has. The "book" was thought to be a verbal history, passed down by a few natives living in the region. I, for one, thought that we had found a city like Machu Picchu or even a Tiwanaku-like settlement, just hidden under the Andes and waiting for the right time to reveal itself. I may have been wrong in this assumption."

"So Doctor," I said, "are we in this 'Ukhu Pacha Tiwanaku' world now?"

"It would appear that way," the Doctor replied.

"This is freaking me out!" Ziggy exclaimed. His accent reflected his stress and for a moment, he sounded like the Taco Bell dog. "I just want to get back to *my* world! The Incans or Bolivians or *whoever* can keep this one!"

"Ziggy's got a point," Doug replied. "We do need to figure a way out of here."

Most of the group had their backs turned to me as they were rummaging through the camp's wreckage. Suddenly, a translucent white being entered the camp near where I was standing, still unseen by the others. It was small and had four legs. It quickly came over to me. I stared for a moment, surprisingly, not scared.

"Yurak?" I said. It was and it was not. As the dog-like spirit did not have a physical form, I just wasn't sure. It wagged its tail and brushed against me.

41

For a moment, I felt a chill run down my spine. He was not physically there; yet I felt him. It was his *spirit*.

In the depths of my being, I thought, *can you hear me boy?* And to my surprise, he answered, *yes*.

Do you understand me, I thought.

Yes, Yurak replied.

Where are we? I asked

You are in my dreams, he said. *I am scared and very glad to see you. I don't see too many friends when I dream.*

I looked down and the ghost Yurak wagged his tail.

"Do you see Yurak?" I asked the others.

Katherine spun around, startled. So did the rest of the group. As they looked at me intently, they saw the ethereal dog at my feet.

"This is Yurak's spirit," I said.

"Come here, boy," Fredrick yelled. The dog did not come. It was almost as if he didn't hear him.

"Yurak, come here," the doctor beckoned. Yurak did not respond.

"Guys, somehow he doesn't respond to words," I said. "However, I can communicate with him."

"*Right!*" Katherine said skeptically.

"You don't understand," I said. "This is Yurak's *spirit* and somehow we are telepathically linked. Yurak is dreaming right now and we are in his dream."

"If he is dreaming, I'd hate to see his nightmares!" Ziggy exclaimed.

About that time Yurak's ears went up and he darted off to the top of a nearby hill. We all followed. He began to whimper and bristle up. *What is it boy?* I asked.

As we all stared at the distant landscape, hazy figures began to appear on the horizon. There were many and they

42

were coming closer. They appeared very distant, but coming our way, nevertheless

Doug quickly grabbed the camera and swapped out the current lens with a long range one to get a better look. His face turned pale, "This can't be good," he said.

"Here, let me see that," I replied.

As I looked through the lens, I saw an army of undead beings. They appeared to be skeletal soldiers; each held a spear. They were drawing closer.

The severity of our situation suddenly became overwhelming because the *fog* was retreating from the marching bones! If that evil death fog was scared of these "people" then I was certain they were something we did not want to tangle with.

"Ghost soldiers?," Katherine said. "Are you being funny again Chuckles?" She had a sense of hope in her voice, and I hated to disappoint her.

"I wish," I said. "Just take a look for yourself."

She gasped and I turned to the others.

"Guys, we've got to get out of here!" I said. "There are ghost warriors coming this way and I seriously doubt they are friendly!"

"Quick," Doctor Francis replied. "Let's head back to the passageway. Perhaps we can evade them if they don't see our retreat!" He frantically began digging through the rubble of the campsite. "I'm looking for anything that we might be able to use as a weapon."

"Check the Jeep!" Ziggy said. "There should be a survival kit there. There will at least be a knife and some equipment we can use."

He was right. In the overturned Jeep, the survival kit was still intact. It was lying upside down in the back seat near the spare tire. He reached in and grabbed it and strapped the knife to his belt. He also found some rope, and handed it to me. "Here, put this in your backpack," he said.

The thought passed through my mind that the knife really wasn't going to do anything to the bones, and you could not kill that which was already dead. I did not say this out loud, because it seemed obvious. At this point, we did not really have a choice.

As we ran up the hill, Fredrick pointed out, "The water was boiling in the passageway. How are we going to get across?"

Great, we'll be boiled like lobsters, or hacked to death by the living dead.

The doctor looked at Fredrick like a deer in headlights. "Uh, I don't..."

"Wait," it was Katherine. "Going back in that hole is not a good idea. We need to find a way to learn about where we are and what has happened *before* starting back."

"I agree," Doug and I both said in unison.

"But first, we need to get out of here," I added.

Lightning flashed in the distance as we climbed higher into the mountains. It would not be long until we made it back to Pabilito's village of death.

"Maybe we can make it to Machu Picchu," Ziggy suggested. "It is pretty popular. There may be some people there." His worried look made it clear that he was not convinced of the validity of his suggestion.

"We're still about 20 kilometers away," Doctor Francis said. He was already out of breath. "That's quite a distance and they are already gaining on us." As the doctor was an older gentleman, I did not see our group running great distances in the high altitudes.

"I'm getting sick," Katherine exclaimed.

"It will be okay," it was Fredrick. "It's the low air and we are all running. Let's get our bearings."

As if he brought it to my attention, I too found myself gasping for breath. *I am like a fish out of water. I just cannot breathe!*

Yurak came up beside me, looking thoughtfully. *Relax.* I closed my eyes and for a moment and I was somewhere else. Yurak and I were standing in a green field somewhere in a lower valley. The sky was blue, the air was pure, and the world was right. *You are in his dream,* I thought. Soon, I was able to breathe again. I opened my eyes and the others had caught their breath as well.

We walked slowly up to the next ridge and looked beyond. Some of the thunderclouds had parted to reveal a volcano belting flames and ash into the sky. *That is the source of the thunder,* I thought. *We weren't looking in this direction before or we would have seen it.*

Yurak began walking up the sulfuric river bed, past Pabilito's village, but not in the direction of the Tomb of the Chief. We had to make a choice: do we follow the ethereal dog or do we take our chances back in the passageway? One thing was for certain, we could not go back to the camp. The ghost warriors would have made it there by now.

"Folks, let's follow Yurak," I proposed, already heading up the riverbed.

"Wait," Doctor Francis objected, "We have no idea where he is going, we should go back to the tomb and hide from those phantoms!"

"I agree with the doctor," Frederick replied.

"Well I'm following the dog," Katherine said.

"Me too," cried Ziggy.

45

"I'm sticking with my friend," Doug also said as he started up the path behind me.

"We need to stick together!" Doctor Francis protested.

"I'm sorry, Doctor," I said, "but I feel Yurak knows something. And that something could keep us safe!"

"We will be in the tomb should you change your mind," the doctor said. "Best wishes to you all."

"And you as well," Doug said.

As the two gentlemen left our view, we continued onwards and upwards along the riverbed, resting our futures on the ethereal Yurak.

CHAPTER 6

"Do you think they'll make it?" It was Katherine. We had been walking for about an hour steadily up the riverbed, none of us saying a word until now.

"I'm not sure," I said. "I only hope the best for them and for us."

Suddenly, Yurak took off running and disappeared ahead of us. I felt a brief moment of panic as he disappeared from view. A minute later he came back and barked at us.

He had left the riverbed and stood at a trail head. Yurak's thoughts were in mine: *It's time for me to wake up, I'll see you soon,* and just like that, he was gone.

The four of us just stood and stared at each other, speechless.

"The dog's gone. Now what?" Doug asked to no one in particular.

"I think he'll be back," I replied, but did not know for sure. *You really blew it this time,* I thought to myself, *you bet all your hopes of getting out of this hellhole on a ghost! Man, what were you thinking!?* I closed my eyes for a moment, trying to clear my head of the negativity. *He'll be back,* I told myself. *At least, I hope so.*

We sat for a moment to rest and eat. Each of us had empanadas in our packs and never could I recall bread tasting so good. I took another swig of water and noticed that my bottle was over half gone. *Be careful there, you definitely don't want to be drinking that orange stuff in the creek bed.*

We resumed our walk along the trail. About forty meters along, the trail bent around to a cliff overlooking the area from which we came. From up here, everything was very small and the danger felt far away. Doug pulled out his camera and took some more pictures.

From this far up, we could barely make out Pabilito's village, but it was there. And, if we looked hard enough, we could see the skull entrance to the Tomb of the Chief. The skeletal army was closer to the Tomb of the Chief, but did not appear to be going specifically to it. It appeared as if both parties were safe from the army's awareness, at least for now.

It also appeared as if we were very close to the mouth of the volcano. Dark clouds seemed very close, I realized. We were very high up the mountain; at the cloud line, in fact.

"If we go down, we'll get killed by phantom Inca soldiers," Katherine said sarcastically. "If we go up, we'll get blown to smithereens."

Just then, the earth began to shake violently and a cloud of ash blew out of the volcano. The eruption was loud – very loud. A large ball of fire shot over the valley in the general direction of Pabilito's village. Lava began oozing over the top edge of the mountain only a few hundred feet above us.

The riverbed was a natural conduit for the lava. Lava began to race down the track, and headed quickly down the very hill that we just climbed, blocking our retreat. *And here I thought the death mist and skeleton armies were our biggest problems.*

"Quickly guys, we've got to get out of here!" I exclaimed.

"We must climb down the volcano's back side!" Ziggy yelled.

In a flash, Ziggy circumnavigated the mountain and began hastily descending the other side. He was going very fast. Ash began falling like evil snow and we tried to keep up.

I could not tell if there was a trail or not, as the ground was covered with ash. It would appear there was a trail, considering the speed at which Ziggy was going.

We followed the treacherous path, stayin as far as possible from the steep cliffs on both sides. Doug was following directly behind Ziggy, with his camera case in one hand, trying to keep his balance with the other.

All of a sudden, Doug lost his footing and began to plummet downwards, and spiraled to the right. His camera case went flying. I frantically reached for my friend, but his momentum quickly carried him down the side of the mountain. He was grabbing for anything that would slow his rolling body. He managed to roll upright and then he stumbled head-over-feet, over the cliff, screaming as he fell to his death a thousand feet below.

"Doug!" I yelled, but it was too late. About twenty feet further down, I found the camera case lying in the ash. I made my way to it and retrieved it. The camera looked intact, the case protecting it, but one could not really tell for sure.

Katherine hugged me there on the cliff. For the first time, I could smell the aroma of bug spray mixed with her sweat as she held me close for a moment. "He was your friend." Looking at me with her deep blue eyes, she said, "I am so sorry."

This would be a nice moment, if circumstances weren't so bad, I thought. Then immediately I felt guilty for even thinking about it. Evil was getting to me, I just knew it.

"We've got to get off here quickly," Ziggy urged. "No time for mourning right now!"

Katherine shot him an angry glance, but he had a point, and with careful footing, we followed Ziggy down the volcano's steep and rugged slope.

The ground shook again and even more ash bellowed out. It was hard to see and even harder to breathe.

About 100 meters down we came across a manmade wall. Following this a little further, Ziggy discovered a door. "In here," he yelled. We darted in.

Just inside the door was a stairway going down. It was very dark and I was skeptical about going down it given our last episode in the Tomb of the Chief.

Looking back out the front, the ash continued to fall. *It's impassable now. You must stay here or descend into darkness.*

There was, however, a very subtle breeze coming from within the belly of the mountain deep below and up the stairway. "Fresh air means there's another entrance!" Ziggy said. I couldn't argue. *Come to think of it, that's the first fresh air I've felt. The outside wind before seemed rancid.*

We fired up the flashlights. All things considered, descending back into the earth was our only option.

The stairs were very narrow, each stone about 6" wide. *Be very careful,* I thought. *One false step and you could wind up like Doug!* This made me both sad and anxious as I put one foot in front of the next. *Down, further down.*

The mountain rumbled with an archaic and unnatural vibration. Sand and gravel from overhead rained down on us. *Stay put,* my mind raced, *don't cave in on us!*

"Oh shit," Katherine said in a panicky voice behind me. "Do you think this was a good idea?"

"I don't really know," I replied.

Just then, we made it to the bottom of the staircase. We were standing in a very large room, not too unlike the one we were in when we first came across the conquistador.

On the far left, lava oozed down the side of the cavern wall. On the right was a walkway with insets every twenty feet or so containing skeletal remains. They were standing upright.

Just below and running alongside the walkway was a freshwater stream. It had started to steam as lava mixed with it.

Lava, death mist, and scary skeletons – what a welcoming party.

"Let us go through the catacombs," Ziggy suggested and started toward the right.

We walked along the passage. It was about four feet wide from the wall to the ledge. The water was about ten feet or so below. As we proceeded further, it got cooler and the breeze picked up. *This is a good thing,* I thought.

Behind us, the cave began to glow as more and more lava poured in. *Better not stay here long.*

Just then, I heard a loud scream. It was Katherine. She was standing beside one of the insets when boney fingers from a skeleton wrapped tightly around her wrist.

It had begun to pull her into the wall.

She was madly trying to fight it off, but it had a death grip on her.

PASSAGEWAY

From behind, I reached for her and successfully grabbed hold of her arm, yanking her free from the skeleton's grasp. Katherine stumbled back into my arms.

I moved toward the inset to get a closer look, but stayed out of its bony arm's reach. I stared for a moment into the skeleton's eye sockets. What I saw sent a shiver down my spine. Where there should have been blank recesses in the skull, I saw a faint and eerie red glow that made my blood run cold. The skeleton stared at me and I subconsciously felt its malevolence. It wanted to make us a part of its damned family.

Katherine grabbed me so tightly I could barely breathe. Her fingernails bit into my flesh as she dragged me quickly onwards and away from the wall.

As I moved away from the demonic skeleton, I felt a sudden, sharp pain in my left shoulder, but I ignored it.

We were now running, Katherine not letting go of me, and Ziggy leading the way. The eye sockets of each of the skeletons on the wall were now glowing just as the first one. *I wonder if they can leave their encasements in the wall,* my mind wildly raced.

Just then, one stepped in front of Ziggy. Without missing a beat, he threw a punch that landed squarely on its jawbone, knocking it to the floor. The skeleton backed off; Ziggy did not. He kicked the creature's midsection, knocking it over the edge of the walkway and into the steaming stream below.

It made a horrible groaning noise as it fell and was soon swept away with the current.

I quickly aimed my flashlight over the edge. The water was very swift. *Funny, I didn't notice it before. I thought it was a quiet underground stream.*

"Behind us!" Katherine screamed.

There were four more of them coming at us.

I will never forget that sight: lava in the background illuminating the skeleton phantoms, their arms outstretched – coming for us!

"Take this!" I said, handing Katherine the camera case that I had been carrying. As soon as it transferred to her hands, I turned around, crunched down like a football player and, with my shoulder down, plowed into the group of skeletons. Excruciating pain shot through my upper arm and shoulder. They all crashed to the ground. I went past them, stumbling, but in the end, retained my balance. Looking back now, I will admit that it was a ballsy move.

Before the first could get up, I grabbed its burial garment and threw it over the edge.

Ziggy quickly followed and likewise grabbed the second being and chucked it over the edge. Katherine stayed back, watching it transpire.

The third one grabbed my leg and started to pull itself up. I uppercut the demon's skull and decapitated it. Again, pain surged across the back of my neck and down my shoulder.

Like some type of macabre soccer match, the skull rolled down the narrow path and struck Katherine – she screamed. In spite of the situation, a strange vision entered my mind of a foreign soccer announcer screaming GOAL!! GOAL!!

The headless skeleton's body continued pulling at me. The beings were surprisingly strong, but they were light. Ziggy grabbed him from behind and threw the headless phantom over the edge.

We both turned and beat the hell out of the fourth and final phantom; its bones flying. We cleared the passage, throwing the remaining bones and debris over the ledge until the passage ahead was clear.

"Now that's some fucked-up shit!" Ziggy said, looking madly around to make sure we had gotten everything and there were no more of them.

When the ordeal was over, I looked down; my knuckles were bleeding. The bones were hard and my flesh was not.

I was nervous. My adrenalin was up. My heart was beating very fast. I tried to shake it off. "We must go on." I said.

"Why are you bleeding?," Katherine looked at me with wide-eyed horror.

"Me?," I asked, and then I felt the pain in my shoulder again. I touched it, afraid to look just yet, and realized that it felt warm, and wet. *That is strange*, I thought.

Then I looked, and almost passed out. My shirt dipped into what looked like a small crater in my shoulder and blood was pouring down my side. Funny what you don't notice when you are fighting for your life.

The skeleton that had Katherine in its bony hands had bitten me. Not a regular human bite, a super skeleton bone-headed bite. It was gross and I felt bad that Katherine had to see me that way. I tried to remain calm. Katherine rushed over to me with a handkerchief and applied pressure. It was at that moment that I decided we were all going to end up like Doug. One way or another, this was hell and this was the end. I would be strong though, for Katherine, for everybody.

CHAPTER 7

A descent into darkness can be maddening. It can drive one insane. I've come to appreciate madness, in all its blissful glory, for I know the "unaware" are uniquely blessed.

Farther along the path, the walkway abruptly ended and there was another set of stairs directly in front of us, going downward. By then, my first flashlight had started to go dim and I knew it would only be a matter of time before I had to resort to my spare.

While descending into darkness is bad enough, being in complete darkness, unable to see what is around you, is terrifying. I immediately wished we had at least one more flashlight.

The stairs went only a few feet down and ended in a pool of water. Carefully studying our choices, I noticed that water was coming into this chamber from three directions. About fifty feet ahead of us, water filled the area from upstream via a water fall. To the left and behind us, was the downstream that followed the path we just traveled. It was very swift and we wouldn't be going that way.

The only other choice was to wade into the pool and follow the upper-right side where the water flowed under some rocks and continued into parts unknown. It too was downstream, but in a direction different from the lava (and skeletons) that we knew lay in the passage just traveled. *Great, more water with rotten corpses in it. I bet they come alive and drown you.* I immediately wished that I had not thought about that.

The cavern in this part had a natural stair-stepping descent and it was as if the path itself had, in fact, turned into the water. *This is wishful thinking. You are only imaging a path where there is none.*

I breathed deeply and realized that fresh air was still coming from further down in front of us. *This must be the way; still on the right track.*

I reached down and touched the water. *Not boiling, that's good; but it's very cold.*

Katherine inspected Doug's camera to make sure it was sealed and secured in the waterproof camera case, and put it in her backpack. She also crammed the conquistador's journal in there as well. "Looks like we're going to get wet," she said. With a step of faith, we all got into the pool and began to wade.

The water was about four feet deep. The cold bit into us. Katherine, standing oh so close, continued to brush against me. As I panned my ever-dimming flashlight, I could not help but notice how the cold made her nipples erect, her perfect breasts accented, as the water swished around them and dampened her lower blouse.

If only we weren't here, I thought to myself, *I might actually enjoy this. It would be nice to daydream right now, to forget this hell we are in and imagine a more pleasant circumstance.* I shook my head and looked away.

Sometimes I think the brain gives us an out when reality is too stressful to cope. Looking back, it was this thought that was my escape during the whole ordeal.

Suddenly the mountain let out another moan and the cavern ceiling began to fall in pieces around us. We hurried along as fast as we could.

Without warning, the area around the waterfall burst open and thousands of gallons of water gushed into the pool.

At once we were swept away, faster and faster into the darkness below. I tumbled; one minute above water and the next minute below; catching my breath between cycles. We were moving so fast.

I blacked out for what seemed like an eternity. Going under, the haunting words of The Doors' Jim Morrison filled my mind: *This is the end, beautiful friend.* And I really thought it was.

The frigid water started to warm up. *Warmer. Warmer still. Where am I?* My mind drifted...

I dreamed that I was somewhere in the tropics. One time, I had gone to Mexico. There is a place there called Xcaret. *It's Mayan, you're not there,* a faint thought protested, but quickly disappeared.

I was floating on a lazy river. I could feel the warm sun on my face and I had not a care in the world.

Looking at the bank, I passed some mangroves. The leaves were vivid shades of green. A gentle breeze blew and one of the leaves came towards me and seemed to float in the air. In the tropical sunlight, I could see salt crystals glistening off the leaf like droplets of rain. *What clarity,* I thought and reached out to touch it. The image disappeared as I tried to close my hands around it.

A dog appeared between some of the branches and began to swim towards me. *I've seen you before,* I thought, still dreaming. *Hi there pup,* I thought.

The dog bumped against me and began pushing towards the mangroves. My feet brushed against the rocks and their underwater branches. *Hey bud, water's shallow here,* I thought.

Get out of the water, it seemed to say to me.

But it's so nice here, I replied.

He barked at me. Loudly. *Okay, I'll get out of the water.*

I started to swim when I realized how heavy the water was and how tired I was. *Ahh... just relax. You don't have to go yet.* The water was so comforting. I was going deeper and deeper under the lazy river.

The root system of the mangroves began to wrap around my feet and legs, pulling me downwards and further into the increasingly warmer water. My head went under and the light of the tropical sun was now far above the surface. It was so dark.

I felt something bite my arm, but not painfully. I was being pulled up by something. *Oh yes, it must be the dog. Nice doggie...* my mind drifted.

The dog dragged me to the shore where I pulled myself up to its banks, reclined my head back and slept.

I don't know how long I was under, but when I opened my eyes, I saw Katherine. She was about an inch away from my face saying, "Wake up!"

I sat up and looked around. No mangroves, no tropical sunlight. It was dark, yet there was a candle-like glow around the room. *Were we in a cave of some sort?* I didn't recognize where we were.

"I thought you were a goner," Ziggy said.

"Yeah," Katherine replied. "The river carried us over a mile and we were separated in total darkness. Yurak showed us where you were and we found you here on the bank."

"Yurak?" I said bewildered. "But he left."

"Well," Ziggy replied. "This might sound odd, but I thought I was lost for good. I was deep in the cave about

300 meters from where you were when I came out of the water.

"I was in total darkness and no longer had my backpack. Yurak appeared out of nowhere and..." he paused. "Well, he seemed to glow and his glow illuminated the area. Like a spirit – but a good one!" He said excitedly.

"He motioned with his neck for me to follow him and ran back to where you and Katherine are now."

"See, he's here now," Katherine said.

Sure enough, the ethereal Yurak was back. He was lying just a few feet away, wagging his tail. He did seem to have a glow about him. *You were in my dream, weren't you boy? You rescued me!* He simply looked, knowingly.

The water gets very hot from here, his thoughts seemed to say to mine. *Keep out of it. Follow me.*

There was a dry area near the cavern wall where part of the ceiling had collapsed as the result of the eruption tremors. Rocks and rubble where scattered about, but it did look as if we could climb our way up the rubble and out of this underground waterway.

Yurak led the way up the rocks and we followed the best we could. There were parts where it was tight. Ziggy squeezed through, with Katherine behind him and me at the tail.

Yurak stopped, bristled up and began to bark madly. *What's going on up front?* I couldn't see a thing.

Just then, Ziggy let out a blood-curling scream.

CHAPTER 8

I discovered that if I closed my eyes and thought about it, I could see what Yurak saw. I'm not sure how, but *somehow* I could.

The ethereal Yurak was facing down a giant snake. The small, coyote-like dog showed its teeth and faced down the larger-than-life predator. The snake lunged at the dog, but went through Yurak and bit Ziggy who was directly behind him.

I opened my eyes just in time to see Katherine slam into me on her retreat out of the hole. I hurried backward myself, but the visions continued.

The giant snake was an anaconda and unlike the other 'undead' beings of this world, this one seemed very much alive and very much agitated. It was over twenty feet long and had deep green scales with black circles which glowed in Yurak's light.

The anaconda wrapped itself around both of Ziggy's legs and threw him to the ground. Yurak jumped on the snake and tried to bite it.

Yurak did not seem to affect the snake and likewise it did not seem to be able to harm the dog. It did, however, afflict much pain on Ziggy.

"My legs!" he cried. Katherine and I could both hear a loud snapping sound as the anaconda broke Ziggy's legs at the kneecaps. "Aaah," he screamed.

The snake reared up, opened its mouth to its widest, and struck down on top of Ziggy's forehead, biting its fangs into his upper forehead and eyes. I have never heard a scream like that in on my life and hope never to again.

Ziggy remembered the knife that he had taken from the Jeep. He pulled it from his belt and drove it into the snake's body that was wrapped around his legs.

The snake momentarily loosened its constriction but at the same time brought its mouth further over Ziggy's head. Ziggy wielded the knife blindly, striking the snake in whatever area he could.

The snake pushed further and now had Ziggy's entire head in its mouth.

"I've got to help him," I told Katherine, and scurried to the top of the grave mound, where I saw the entire picture.

Ziggy was an undistinguishable mass writhing within the anaconda's grip. I could barely make out the knife, which Ziggy had now dropped in hopeless desperation, as he tried to get his hands between the snake's mouth and his neck. The blood that poured out of his neck and over his shoulders was horrifying.

I grabbed the knife and made a purposeful cut at the snake's upper region just above where I thought Ziggy's head to be. I hit the mark and continued cutting around the snake's head until it was completely severed from the rest of its body. As its life oozed out, the snake was finally limp.

Ziggy's body fell lifelessly to the ground. I was too late. I stood in sheer horror, not knowing what to do. Yurak stood there barking at the snake, but eventually came to the same conclusion that I had – the worst of it was over.

"Kill me," a voice I didn't recognize said. "Hurry, do it now!" What was happening? It took me a full minute to realize it was Ziggy.

Oh my God he isn't dead, I thought.

I could barely look at him but I had to make sure that I was not crazy. I looked down and saw Ziggy covered in blood, looking at me with pleading eyes. I could tell that he was not going to make it. The blood that was pouring from his body told me that he must be suffering terribly. The thing that didn't make sense was that his blood had started to clot, and the bleeding was stopping. Was he healing? No, I decided, the evil place was just prolonging his death.

"End it," Ziggy pleaded again. The bleeding had stopped, but you could see it moving under his skin, like it was filling his body cavity. I hesitated. *Could he be healing?*

He let out a cry at that point that was so horrible it made the decision for me. I knew I had seconds before Katherine came up the rubble, I had to act. I felt numb as I took the knife in my hand and brought it straight down into Ziggy's jugular. I could not watch, but I felt the knife go in. *What a horrible fate for him, this can't be real.*

Katherine came into the area very reluctantly and realizing what had happened cried, "Oh God no! Not Ziggy!"

"What are we going to do?" she pleaded.

"I don't know," I choked out, the words just wouldn't come. "I want this nightmare to end." I felt very guilty for what I had just done. I knew that it was the best thing for Ziggy. Who knew how long the horrible place would keep him alive and suffering; even worse, how long until he would have been torn apart by skeletons?

Yurak barked again and started to move further up the mound of rubble.

Up ahead, we saw daylight. Well, it actually wasn't "daylight" but rather that surreal twilight that I've come to know from this eerie world.

The narrow crack in the earth that we had been crawling through opened up, and Katherine and I found ourselves at the bottom of a large hole – a sinkhole to be exact. The walls looked to be over a hundred feet high, very steep, but not unclimbable. Even though we were in a hole, I was much relieved to at least see daylight, considering the ordeal with the snake.

Around the floor of the sinkhole were broken boards and a tremendous amount of debris. A great deal was in a pile on one side of the floor, a few feet from where our opening emerged. *Someone's house must have been over the hole when it collapsed,* I thought.

A very faint cry could be heard coming from the pile. Katherine and I looked at each other, horrified.

Yurak bristled up. *What's below the pile, boy?* I thought.

He simply barked. Given the encounter with the anaconda, it was best not to take chances.

The cry grew louder and begun to echo in the cave: *ñak'ariy.* A few moments later: *ñak'ariy.*

"Suffering," Katherine said.

"What?"

"Suffering," she replied, "ñak'ariy is Quechan. It means 'to suffer.'"

We were all suffering this day: *First Doug, then Ziggy. And what about Pabilito and his wife? And his children!?* "Oh, shit!" I said horrified.

The boards began to move.

Ñak'ariy - ñak'ariy - ñak'ariy.

"What is it?" Katherine asked.

"Remember the wash basin?"

"What?"

"The wash basin, damn it! The one with the hand!"

"Yes?!"

"Well, Ziggy said that Pabilito had six kids. One was chopped up and lying in the basin. Where were the others?"

Ñak'ariy - ñak'ariy - ñak'ariy.

I began to look at the pile, running around it frantically. Sure enough, I could make out pieces of the thatch work roofing and the old rotten wood. "Shit! This is Pabilito's house. It must have fallen in the sinkhole!" *Somewhere under it, all those dead kids are coming back to life! They are coming for you.*

The voices grew louder and louder.

Ñak'ariy - ñak'ariy - ñak'ariy!

"We've got to climb out of this hole!" I said.

Yurak barked and dove into the rubble. He yelped and came back up.

"Oh my God!" Katherine said. "He's carrying a hand!"

Without wasting time, we began to scale the wall freestyle.

Yurak dropped the hand and resumed barking at the rubble.

Body parts began to swirl around the bottom of the sinkhole like an angry tornado forming itself into Frankenstein-like zombie children. First one, then another, then another. These child-like figures, once assembled, plunged on the dog. He yelped.

Unlike the snake encounter, Yurak was able to feel the attacks from the child-zombies. They clawed at him and ripped at his fur.

He broke free and jumped in a supernatural leap to the top of the sink hole. It was so quick, I almost didn't see it happening. *How could he jump so high?* I thought to myself.

Suddenly, I could hear the sounds of the child zombies scurrying up the cavernous walls. *Better hurry... they're on their way!*

"Quick!" Katherine shouted. "They're coming after us!"

We had made it three-quarters of the way up the wall when the first zombie reached Katherine. "Mama," it moaned!

"Yikes!" Katherine screamed as she kicked at it.

Her boot landed squarely on the zombie child's forehead and he shrieked and plummeted into the darkness below.

In a split-second she passed me and made it to the top with lightning speed. I quickly followed.

A few seconds later, a zombie girl emerged from the sinkhole. I kicked her in the stomach and she flew back and over the precipice.

I looked at Katherine in utter terror. The sinkhole began to moan with the sounds of undead children.

One after another, they began to emerge and one by one, we fought them back over the edge.

I began to look around. Yurak had again disappeared and lava was all around. It was as if we were standing on an island in a lake of fire, with parts of the landscape jutting up here and there. The conquistador's words flooded my mind: *I have made it back, across the Lake of Fire, across the Plains of Death only to realize that I cannot escape.*

I wasn't sure if it was the glow of the lava, but when I looked at Katherine's face, something about her eyes glowed. They changed. It was eerie and almost wolf-like.

"Run," she growled. "I don't care where. Just go! I will find you!" She heaved her pack at my chest and I caught it in surprise. With that, she threw her arms back and let out a howl.

"What the f..." I started to say, but then realized that I probably should heed her advice. I took off running across the broken landscape – ash and lava all around. I did not look back until I was about 100 yards or so. I stopped momentarily to catch my breath and get my bearings.

Katherine was still at the edge of the sinkhole. Her body was convulsing. I had never seen anything like it. She shook and howled again.

I watched in amazement as the figure changed before my eyes. I felt that I truly was insane, as I could not believe what I was seeing.

Katherine's face became elongated, her beautiful nose transforming into a snout, and fangs appeared from her mouth. She threw herself on the ground and her body twisted and contorted with bulging muscles. She began ripping at her clothes.

Her back arched like a cat; but it was no cat busting from the seams of her shirt. Down on all fours, she howled again. It was deafening.

Before my very eyes, Katherine the linguist-translator, my fantasy love, and my partner in this ordeal, became a werewolf.

To my horror I didn't know whether to be really turned on, or terrified for my life. *Why would you be turned on by a beautiful woman's body being ripped apart as she turned into a wolf?* This place was making me crazy.

I ran and ran and ran; unsure of what I witnessed, unsure of anything in this macabre world. My lungs burned from the limited oxygen in the high altitude combined with the ash spewing from the volcano.

At some point, I realized I was about to faint. I could not tell if I was hallucinating, but I was near the Tomb of the Chief, as its foreboding skull entrance appeared in front of me. That was the last thing I remember before hitting the dirt at the opening of the tomb.

In my mind's eye, I could hear, or more precisely *feel* myself being surrounded by the zombie children from the sinkhole. They made it out. Somehow, they would be forever in my nightmares. *Is this the end?* I wondered.

Perhaps so, my mind countered. *Perhaps they will turn you into one of them, perhaps...*

I just couldn't wake up. Somewhere in the distance, I heard screams. Blood curling screams.

In my foggy mind, I knew those were the screams of the zombie children. The wolf had them and she devoured them until there was silence.

I don't know how long I laid there in the dirt, unable to breath, unable to move. My world was spinning.

I do know that at some point, the wolf had found me. I could feel her on top of me. I knew if I could only open my eyes, I would see her staring at me, ready to devour me like she had devoured those apparitions.

I could smell her fur, definitely that of animal, but faintly reminiscent of the way Katherine smelled. I knew in my blacked-out state the wolf only needed to open its mouth and rip my throat out. She was that close.

I could feel her muzzle only inches from my nose. I sensed her breath. I waited for the worse.

The wolf grunted and began nudging me. She began licking my face, like a friendly dog. For a moment, I thought it might be Yurak, but I was too afraid to open my eyes and find out. I smelled blood on her breath; I knew she wasn't a dog. I simply laid very still and waited on my fate.

When I did finally open my eyes, it was not the wolf, but Katherine who was beside me, huddled and naked. She was covered in dirt and visibly shaken. Had this been any other circumstance, she would have looked like a woodland creature, possibly an elf or nymph from mythology, but I knew what I saw and what she was.

"We need to talk," she said.

CHAPTER 9

Damn, she's beautiful. Even covered in dirt, I found it difficult to keep my eyes turned away as she spoke.

"I'm sorry you had to find out this way," she said. "I had hoped no one would ever find out. But given the circumstances, I felt it was necessary."

"This is too much for my mind to comprehend," I said.

"I understand. The Change affects me only during full moons or in times of dire trouble. The wolf protects me."

"I never believed in werewolves. I thought they were only legend," I said.

Katherine continued, "I am over 200 years old and was changed in Spain."

"But you only look twenty-something!" I interjected.

"True," she said. "I was studying Castilian Spanish in Madrid. It was very late one night. I was walking back home from the university when it appeared."

She continued, "At first, I took it to be a large dog. It looked like a German shepherd, but it was too big to be one. Its ears were pulled back and its teeth..." Katherine shuddered, "I'll never forget it.

"I ran as hard as I could, but it was faster. It was on me before I knew it. It began biting me and I thought I was going to be torn limb from limb.

"Fortunately, there was a policeman who heard me screaming. He shot it and it ran off." She stared into the distance for a moment.

"It took me weeks to recover. I almost died from loss of blood. Then one night, under a full moon it happened."

I glanced back at her and then pulled my gaze away.

"I experienced the Change for the first time. At first, it was uncontrollable. I was crazy. When the Change took me, I blacked out only to wake up hours later, completely naked like I am now, with the taste of blood in my mouth and faint memories of what I had done.

"Over the years, I learned to accept who I was and gradually became more aware of my wolf. I can change at will, but it is always painful."

"Did you force your change just a bit ago?" I asked.

"Yes. Despite the grave danger we were in before, there were always several of us to take care of it. Finally, it was just you and me. I had to even the odds, even if it meant exposing my *other* nature to you."

"I am speechless," I said. And I really was.

"Had we been in the real world and not this alter-universe or whatever it is, I would have held back. The stakes are just too high now and I realized we are in a fight for our lives here. My wolf will not stand down in the face of such grave danger any longer."

I looked back at her and could see the wolf in her eyes, just under the surface.

"If we are to survive this," she continued, "I must change back to the wolf. I need to scout the territory and know what we are up against. As a wolf, I can more than hold my own."

Quite frankly, I didn't know what to think. Was I to go with her – being changed in werewolf form – and hope that she didn't turn me into her next meal once she got hungry? How much control did she have over her "other" nature?

As if reading my thoughts, she said, "You can stay here if you wish and I will return once I learn more. To be honest, I am not sure if you are safer with me or alone."

"If I move from this location," I said, "how will you find me?"

"The wolf's sense of smell is very good and I have learned to develop it over the years." She paused. "Although, I will say the ash blowing around and covering the ground is making it very difficult for me to track.

"I do know of another way," she said, a wolfish grin on her face. "If we mate, we will be bonded and I can find you anywhere. I won't have to rely solely on scent, even if you move to another location."

I finally allowed my eyes to fully take in her beauty. It was true that I was attracted to her, but the circumstances were so off-kilter, so unreal. Should I bond with a wolf?

She sat up from her huddled position so that I could fully behold her. "Ever make love to a werewolf?" She asked.

With that, I came to her with an animal-like impulse. I have never experienced such heat before. Her she-wolf scent filled my nostrils with a musk that drew me into her embrace. Her eyes flashed the wolf again and she let them stay that way.

The twisted, hell-bent world in which we found ourselves disappeared for a moment. The experience filled my senses in a way which no other had. I felt her wolf as she dug claws into my back, the pleasure intensifying as I felt her spirit intertwined with mine.

Her face began to change into the wolf again and with an unexpected lurch, she/it bit into my shoulder with a sharp pain and intensity that was mixed with the pleasure we were experiencing. The orgasm was immediate and breathtaking.

When it was over she whispered, "Poor baby," and gently kissed the side of my neck.

My shoulder pounded and noticed a trickle of blood from where the bite marks were. "I like it rough and all, but my shoulder hurts like hell!"

At least she had bit into my "good" shoulder. This pain was much more bearable. I was disgusted with myself for what I had just let happen. She was an animal, and a very old animal at that. What the fuck was going on in my life? I wanted her even now, knowing that she wasn't the sweet beautiful woman that I had become attracted to. Now I figured out what it was that drew me to her, animal magnetism. This was one screwed up situation, and despite all the death that had surrounded us I was enjoying myself.

She intimately looked at me and said, "Now I can see you, if I try, no matter where you are."

I pondered this revelation for a moment as she continued, "Mates bond for life. Sometimes it is telepathic, sometimes it is with emotion. Although we do not know each other well, we are in a fight for our lives and somehow my wolf feels this was right. We must survive this ordeal."

It made mad-sense, and based on the events of the day, I could not argue. Thinking about this, I added, "I felt something remarkable, I just can't describe it."

"Yes, I felt it too."

"Your wolf terrifies me, but yet I am strangely drawn to you."

"The wolf is both a monster and a curse, but I have come to accept that. At rare times, however, it is a blessing and it may be what protects us both in this dire circumstance that we have found ourselves."

"What do we do next?" I asked, not sure if I expected an answer.

"When you ran, I followed your trail back to the tomb's entrance. Strangely, this is where we started."

"I really wasn't sure where I was going," I admitted, a bit embarrassed. "I saw you become that wolf and I thought I might be your next meal!"

She grinned. "That was probably wise. Had it been a hundred years earlier, I would not have cared. I had very little control over the beast within. Now, we experience each other consciously. I don't lose control as often."

I don't lose control as often, I thought to myself. *I hope to hell I don't ever make her mad or am near her when she does lose control.*

As if sensing my thoughts, she said, "Don't worry, a wolf doesn't usually eat her mate."

I stared at her with both astonishment and amazement.

"What? Didn't think I could read your mind?," Katherine said. "I can now. And for better or worse, you will be able to sense me too, as we have bonded." She paused and added, "The three of us."

"You, me, and the *wolf*?" I asked.

"Yes. Now I must change. I cannot speak when I am in wolf form, however, I still should be able to communicate with you through thought."

With that, she backed up, turned and started sprinting. Slightly different than before, she changed as she ran. She and the wolf became one supernatural creature and then she was gone, disappearing in the distance at a pace that I could not even hope to follow.

Once she disappeared from sight, I felt incredibly empty, *and alone.* A wave of panic swept through me and I fought the urge to hold it down. *Don't leave!* My panic-stricken mind cried out.

As if at once, I heard her in my head. *No worries, we are here and on the hunt. Stay put.*

And with that, I sat back and waited.

CHAPTER 10

I had to really fight to block out the thought that at any minute some unwelcomed creature from this unholy world would come upon me and it would be all over. Would it be a skeleton warrior, a giant snake, zombies? What could be next? I shuddered at the thought.

I waited for what seemed like hours. At times I closed my eyes, only for a moment, for I feared my peril should I doze off. However, during these times, I would catch glimpses as if looking through the eyes of something else. *Katherine's wolf,* I thought to myself. *Somehow, the bond she described allowed me to see through her eyes if I concentrated.*

I saw, in my mind's eye, a plateau in a far-off place. The plateau was covered in grass that was unlike the rocky desolation where I was now hiding. She had stopped moving and appeared to be watching this highland from afar.

There were not-quite-human figures in the far distance. I say this because they were very short in stature, yet their bodies were broad and muscular. They were similar to a dwarfs, but not quite. They appeared to be herders or nomads. There were also four-legged creatures in great number around their camps. The wolf's vision was keen, but because of the distance, I could not gather if these creatures were goats or something else.

A great hunger rose through me. *Am I really that hungry?* I thought to myself. *No, it is the wolf. Katherine is very hungry. Those goats would make a very yummy meal. No, she was looking at the nomads,* I shuddered at the thought. I decided to pretend she wanted the goats and the nomads were just in the way.

For a moment, my mind recalled what I witnessed at the sinkhole. I shuddered at the thought and opened my eyes momentarily to break the link.

I looked down at Katherine's pack, thinking of how it was important to her that she entrust me with it prior to the change. *I wonder what you've got in it,* I thought, and then remembered that she had stored the conquistador's journal in the pack along with Doug's camera.

I carefully removed the centuries-old book and examined it in the eerie light of this world. Back in the passageway, we had only looked at the end of the man's writings. I thumbed back several pages and read some more, hoping to gain insight to the ill-fated ordeal of the Spanish soldier...

19 September 1530

The Andean air is very shallow at this altitude. Many of my men have succumbed to illness and fatigue. I am certain it is the air.

We have made much progress in our quest to rid the region of Capac and his army of heathens, with our latest victory occurring today.

The natives had established a trading post in a field where we are camping now. They called this marketplace Leng. There were many farmers here with all sorts of fruits, vegetables, sheep, and goats.

At first, we did not know if they would be friendly, but word had reached them previously from Capac and even the simple farmers took up the fight against us.

They fought well, with ferocity in fact, but ultimately were no match for our skills and swordsmanship. The fight lasted seven hours and in the end, we were victorious.

We killed off all men, women, and children. We gathered as much produce as was possible to carry and corralled the livestock into a nearby barn for harvesting once we had dealt with the Capac business.

Something I did find journal worthy was a small white dog that the natives used to herd the livestock. Up until now, I had not seen very many dogs here in the Andes. At first, I thought it might be a mongrel and almost killed it on sight, but after seeing how it herded the animals, thought it might be useful to us.

Interesting, I thought as I looked up from reading to rest my eyes for a moment. Translating the Spanish handwriting to English seemed to tire my eyes. Of course, it could be the weird light of this world.

As I stared around the desolate wasteland in which I sat, I briefly heard a noise that sounded like a flute. *Just my imagination,* I told myself. I concentrated and heard it again.

It wasn't really music as much as just random notes played in an incomprehensible order. At once, the flute was silent.

I moved from my hiding place to get a better look at where the sound was coming from. As I stood up, I discovered I was only thirty feet away from a tall man cloaked in a black robe.

In the twilight sky, I could not make out his face, only his height. He was not looking at me, but rather had his head tilted in a way indicating that he was also listening to the flute. I was not certain, but it looked that way.

He turned to me and began to approach. I was afraid, but his gait did not look threatening.

"There you are," he said. He spoke in plain English, though my disoriented mind also thought he spoke in a different language all together, and only I understood it.

Keeping his distance, the stranger spoke again. "Most people travel in spirit to this world. But I see you've made it physically and in one piece."

I felt a lump in my throat and for a moment, I did not know if I could talk. As if sensing my hesitation, the stranger continued.

"I am Nyarlathotep and you would be wise not to stay here long."

"I... I am not sure how we got here." I managed to get out.

"You came through a soul portal on an autumnal equinox." Nyarlathotep said matter-of-factly. "Because of the exact time you came through the portal, you managed to make the trip in flesh, not simply spirit." He took a step forward. I still could not make out his face. It was like his body was that of a human, but he was faceless, shrouded in darkness.

Well there it was. It seemed a simple enough explanation for everything that had happened. How often in a situation as dire as this does a man in black come to you and tell you exactly what is going on? I should be glad; now I knew why we were here, and somehow I knew that this must have been what happened to the conquistador. The bad thing was, things did not go very well for him.

"Can I go back?" I asked.

"Yes and no." Nyarlathotep continued, "You definitely cannot go back the way you came. It is a one-way journey."

He tilted his head again, as if listening for that imaginary flute. "You'll definitely want to get your partners out of the hole; they won't survive much longer."

I instantly remembered Dr. Francis and Fredrick, having split from our group to journey on their own.

"There is only death down there, as this world only welcomes the dead," Nyarlathotep said.

I gulped, "Then how do we get out?"

"I can help you, but I want your wolf as payment."

My mind riveted back to Katherine. "I do not know where she is," I said.

"Of course you do," Nyarlathotep said angrily. "She is on the plains of Leng, sizing up her next meal. I enjoyed her display of brutality towards the young ones.

"Bring her to me and I will open up the portal to your world and let you," he pointed towards the Tomb of the Chief, "and your friends down there, return to that plane from which you came."

He paused as if for effect, "Of course, that is if you hurry up and get them out of there." He added, "I do like your wolf. She would do nicely for a pet."

I shivered at the thought. Could I leave Katherine here in this world to be this *thing's* pet? I didn't think I could.

She would be able to take care of herself, I thought. *I would not. Evil, there it was again, creeping into my head and making me think crazy. She saved me, why would I do that to her. Besides she was my mate now, and I didn't know what, but that meant something.*

"Come to me when she returns," Nyarlathotep commanded. "My steed is nearby. He will deliver you to me when the time comes."

With that, he disappeared.

I cannot explain it adequately, but I felt a terrible emptiness inside that the words I write here cannot describe. For many moments, there was no sound, only emptiness. I felt lost and did not know what to do next.

I tried closing my eyes to see Katherine, but she too seemed very far away and our link was only a dim fraction of what it was before Nyarlathotep's visit. *I miss you,* was all I could think to say across the void of consciousness. I was not sure if she could hear me. It was only with hope that I gathered up the strength for what I had to do next.

With sheer might and determination, I reentered the Tomb of the Chief.

CHAPTER 11

The tomb was *a lot* different than I remembered. The walls were chiseled into triangular patterns that seemed to glow in an unnatural green light. A rat scurried by that was larger than a cat. It tried to nip at me and I kicked it away. It made a noise that was part squeal and part hiss, stared at me with dark, beady eyes, and then retreated into some unknown place beyond.

I pictured a hundred more of those nasty creatures feasting on the remains of our fallen comrade. The vision implanted itself into my brain. I never would have pictured such a thing before this ungodly mission to escape Hell.

Unlike the last time I entered, this passageway appeared to be carved out of solid rock. In the faint glow, I could see hundreds, if not thousands, of human skulls and various bones littered throughout. Passage through the corridor was impossible without stepping on them.

How many people had accidentally wandered into this wasteland? How was it possible that they met the exact same unfortunate coincidence that we did? I began to feel completely out of control of my life again.

I moved forward uneasily as the ancient bones crunched underfoot. Quickly, the ceiling became shorter and shorter until I could not proceed forward unless crawling on all fours.

As I was about to place my hands into the bones beneath me, I decided to yell out for Fredrick and Dr. Francis, to avoid having to proceed any further.

"Hello!" I yelled. "Is anyone down there?"

My voice echoed over and over. I listened, but heard nothing. I proceeded about ten feet further and called out again. Something slithered across my left hand, and I tried not to think about it.

I moved another ten feet and the room opened up a bit. I looked around and the green glow illuminated what appeared to be a gallery of sorts. Ancient paintings adorned the walls. In the center of the room stood a solitary stone tablet with various geometric shapes engraved into it which emitted a faint yellow glow that contrasted with the green light from the crystals above. The brightest glowing shape that I could make out on the tablet was a picture of an obelisk.

In the strange light, the paintings on the walls were life-like, as their colors raised three-dimensionally from the very stone on which they were painted. As I studied one in particular, it seemed to move and take on a life of its own. *My mind must be playing tricks on me,* I thought anxiously.

It was a reptile, possibly an alligator or crocodile that didn't quite resemble those that I had seen. Its limbs were longer, like that of a rhino. Its tail was a stub and not much of a tail at all. But the most peculiar thing about this creature was its head. It was abnormally big, perhaps indicating intelligence, but I could not be sure. The head was long and full of razor-sharp teeth and its entire body was covered in scales.

In my fascination, I watched the creature in the painting begin to move ever so slightly. It lifted one of its forearms to reveal hands like that of a human, only much thicker and larger. Upon close inspection, the fingers were adorned with rings and gems. I watched it raise its 'hand' and lower it again.

I pulled my gaze away and looked around.

The chamber was about thirty feet wide and stretched an unknown distance ahead of me. Remembering Nyarlathotep's warning that my friends would perish if they stayed down here, I couldn't help but wonder how long I should tarry here.

I called out again. This time, I heard a faint answer.

"We're down here," the voice called back. It was Dr. Francis.

"Guys, you've got to get out of here quick!" I announced.

About five minutes later, the two came crawling towards me. "Look what I found," Frederick explained excitedly. He held up something red and sparkly.

"It's a ruby!" he exclaimed as he handed it to me for inspection.

Sure enough, I held in my hands a large ruby, possibly ten karats or more. I smiled and handed it back.

"Good heavens, boy!" Dr. Francis exclaimed. "Have you been attacked by a wild animal or something?" I could tell he was referring to my torn-up shoulder and my overall grimy appearance from crawling around on the cave floor.

"It's a long story." I replied. "But guys, we need to get back to the surface right away."

"You don't understand," countered Dr. Francis. "The entire floor is covered with gems like the one Frederick has. We should collect as many as we can."

"I understand their value and don't doubt there are many," I argued. "But listen, something terrible has happened. Doug and Ziggy are both dead and Katherine, has . . . changed." I wasn't quite ready to tell them that she changed into a werewolf and felt it best to let them first deal with the shock of the deaths of our colleagues before they questioned my sanity with the werewolf claim.

"What do you mean, she's 'changed'?" Fredrick asked.

"I'll explain later, but first we need to get out of here. We're in great danger if we don't get our asses back to the surface!"

"Explain?" Asked Dr. Francis.

"I just had a conversation with this..." I paused, *What was he actually?* "This thing called Nyarlathotep and he said you will surely die if you stay down here."

Dr. Francis' face turned pale white and he looked like a ghost in the dimly lit green chamber. "Did you say 'Nyarlathotep?'"

"Yes, that is what he said his name was."

"God save us all. We best heed his warn—"

Before he could get out the last part of his word, one of the alligator creatures from the wall murals pounced down in front of us – suddenly alive! It bit at Fredrick, but missed.

I could tell that other murals were starting to come to life. Rather than wait for the other two, I hauled ass back the way I had come.

Fredrick and the doctor were quick to follow. The alligator creature was not very fast, seeming to be encumbered by its jewelry of all things. Nevertheless, it was following us up through the chamber.

We almost made it when the thing stood up on its hind legs, grabbed a skull from the floor of the passageway and threw it at Fredrick with the skill and force of a major league baseball player.

It cracked Fredrick on the head, sending him sprawling to the cavern floor. Blood burst from his nose, yet he picked himself up, fear and adrenalin fueling his return to our hasty retreat.

We worked our way back up and out of the passage. At some point, the alligator creature stopped its pursuit. When we finally reached the exit, we emerged back into the same pseudo-world that we had left, twilight sky and all. I had secretly hoped that we would be back in the real world, but my optimism was short-lived.

We stood for a moment and brushed ourselves off. Fredrick was noticeably dazed. His hair was matted with blood and his nose continued to bleed.

"Please turn around and let me see you, Fredrick," Dr. Francis said.

As Fredrick turned, we could both see that the skull the alligator threw was somehow embedded into the back of Fredrick's skull, its mouth attached to the back as if it had bitten him in the back of the head.

Dr. Francis carefully took the skull, pried its mouth open, and pulled it out of Fredrick's head, shaking and cursing as he worked. "This fucker is going to get infected, you know."

After Fredrick was tended, Dr. Francis turned to me, took me by the hand, looked right in my eyes and said, "Please, describe Nyarlathotep to me."

I explained that he was a very tall man. *Was 'man' the right word? I guess it would work.* He was probably seven feet tall and wore a black robe.

"Please describe his face," said the doctor.

I had to think hard. "Actually, I could not see his face." I said. "He was wearing a hood, but I could not make out any of his features."

"Was his face empty?" pressed the doctor.

"That's sort of a weird word to describe it, but yes. It was like I was staring into blackness."

"No!" Dr. Francis erupted. "This is very, very bad for us!"

"Doc, you're freaking me out," Fredrick said. He was examining his ruby in the eerie light of this world while at the same time wiping his bloody nose with a handkerchief. *The ruby is the same color as Fredrick's bloody nose and head*, I thought to myself.

The doctor continued: "There is a story in an ancient necromantic text that talks of an empty space – a desert – where a faceless man walks the earth. But this was not an ordinary man; he was a god in human form.

"It is rumored that he only deals with those he chooses and is murderously impatient, swiftly killing those who bore him.

"Sir," Dr. Francis said looking at me. "You have looked upon the Chaos that Crawls and have spoken with the devil himself!"

"Oh, boy," I said loudly. "I'm not sure why I am still here then or why he even bothered talking with me."

"You must be a conduit!" Dr. Francis exclaimed. "That must be why he spared your life. You represent a link between the world of the dead and that of the living!"

"I'm not the only one he is fascinated with. He has a keen interest in Katherine and knows where she is."

Fredrick and the Doctor both exchanged a glance that told me at once they knew something more than they were saying.

20 September 1530

My dreams have started to become so bizarre. Last night at camp, I dreamed I saw the white dog carrying a flute, circling our campfire. He eventually jumped up on a nearby stump and began playing a strange melody that I could not quite pick out.

One by one, the men started dancing to this tune and as they danced, their bodies started to convulse uncontrollably. I stared in horror, but knowing it was just a dream, watched with utmost fascination as they danced to the dog's song.

The strange movements of my men looked like those of a puppet. It was as if their limbs were being manipulated by an imaginary puppet master who was forcing their every move.

As if they had lost their minds, each man started wailing and clawing at his clothing, as if something was itching him. They ripped at their garments and continued to scratch until their skin began to bleed and come off.

I felt my face become wet and for a moment wondered if I too was scratching at my face, when I awoke abruptly to find the white dog licking at my face. I immediately realized it was all just a terrible dream.

I miss the olden days back in Spain. I long for my homeland and hope that the Queen will welcome us back after this quest has been completed.

PASSAGEWAY

21 September 1530

We have made much progress today. The white dog has proven to be a valuable asset. Our scout Christopher noticed the dog following a trail deep into the jungle and after a few hours discovered that the dog was actually following Cupac's men, just as we were. Perchance this dog belonged to one of these heathens, but I cannot be certain.

Christopher followed the dog and eventually discovered where they were camped. He reports several men gathered outside an entrance to a jungle cave. Of peculiar note, the orifice has been carved to resemble a giant human skull.

Our battle plan should be relatively simple: we will blockade the entrance and wait them out. By trapping them inside, we can kill them one by one as they attempt to leave.

23 September 1530

After two long days, not a soul appeared from within their stronghold. Our men decided it best to venture into the jungle cave and have a look at their defenses. Upon entering the tunnel, we quickly became disoriented.

None of the enemy forces were immediately noticeable. We pushed onward into the darkness and the narrow passageway opened up into a large circular room.

It was almost as if we were inside a giant ceremonial chamber. Equally spaced at twelve points around the circle, a triangle was etched into the floor.

We were somewhat alarmed to say the least! The etchings glowed faintly in some unnatural manner. They pulsed from darker to bright, as if the room itself were a living thing!

In addition to the floors, the walls and ceiling were made up of some alien architecture that I had never seen in any of my previous travels. It was as if the very room itself was carved from solid crystal.

Everywhere we looked we saw triangular patterns etched into the walls. Staring at the pattern for too long, one could become very ill, as it bothered the eyes due to the multitude of the triangles. I have sketched a tiny part of the pattern here lest I forget it later.

PASSAGEWAY

Except the way we came, we could not find any other exit from the room. What kind of deviltry was this? Where did Capac and his men go?

We were determined to find out and began studying the walls at length. As I had feared, several of my men became violently ill from the visual stress of examining the wall of patterns.

I felt it best that we retreat back to the surface and see if we could determine an alternate escape route that the enemy forces used.

We retreated in haste, as the enemy had already gotten over a two-day head start due to our procrastination in attempting to wait them out.

Emerging from the cave, my forces were baffled at the strange world we stepped into. We were in both shock and disbelief. The jungle that we thought we would be returning to was now a desert!

CHAPTER 12

We hurriedly walked a good 100 meters or so to put some distance between us and the passageway's entrance, just in case the alligator creatures emerged. All of us watched carefully and waited.

I looked over at Fredrick and could not help but wonder how much blood he lost or was losing, as the neck wound looked much worse than his nosebleed.

Blood trickled down his neck from the wound the skull baseball had made. In fact, his neck was covered in blood and looked as if he had been dipped in a deep crimson paint. Fredrick Gonzalez almost looked like he could pass as a native himself.

As we faced the cave, a noise that sounded like a horse came from the valley behind us. Nyarlathotep's words came rushing back to my mind. *My steed is nearby. He will deliver you to me when the time comes.*

I wasn't sure what I expected to see, however the sight I beheld filled me both with astonishment and horror.

A horse-like creature was facing the lava-filled valley with its tail to us. From a distance, it reminded me of the Pegasus creature from Greek mythology, only darker and more macabre.

It had wings like that of a dragon or large bat. Its skin was like night, or more precisely, like the color of shadows. It was like the color of a crow, only instead of light reflecting from its wings, it absorbed light and stood in a self-emitting shadow.

It had four legs like a horse, but instead of hooves, its feet were talons – a mix of both claws and massively large hands.

But if all of this was not peculiar enough, as it turned upon hearing our approach, I was shocked to see that it had no fur. Unlike a horse of our world, its skin resembled that of rotting flesh – its hairless hide in a perpetual state of decomposition! This was no horse, no Pegasus, but a night "mare" in the truest sense of the word – a corpse steed to be more precise.

As it faced us, its eyes glowed with a terrifying bluish light. It made a blow sound, followed by a nicker. It watched us from a distance but did not approach.

My two companions looked like they were about to run, when I said to them, "Stay, I don't think it will harm us."

"What do you mean?" asked the doctor.

"This corpse steed belongs to Nyarlathotep and he is waiting for us."

"What the fuck!" cried Fredrick.

I couldn't refrain any longer; I had to tell these men about Katherine. "Listen, you both may think I have lost my mind, but Katherine is a werewolf and she is alive, but not here."

The doctor squinted at me very seriously but did not interrupt my explanation.

I continued, "We were in the fight of our lives. We had been trapped in a sinkhole and as we climbed out of it, we were followed by some unknown number of – *what the hell were they exactly* – zombies. Katherine changed right before my eyes, told me to run, and fought them off in beast form.

"She emerged victorious and explained everything to me once we were safe."

"But where is she now?" inquired Fredrick, who was rubbing his head and looking at his hand to see if there was still blood coming from it.

"She changed back into a werewolf and is out in the plains of Leng, scouting the territory."

"Leng is a good day's journey from here," remarked Doctor Francis. "How do you even know where she is?"

"Nyarlathotep told me," I said, and then added, "Plus, I can sense her."

"I believe it is time for you to learn the truth," said Doctor Francis. "Katherine is part of our pack. In fact, both of us are werewolves. I am the alpha and leader. Mr. Gonzalez here is also one of us and my first in command."

Well why the hell did that surprise me? Of course they are all werewolves! I am the only normal one left and that's up for debate since I am a conduit to Katherine's spirit. And truthfully speaking, I do not know if you would call being a telepathically linked spirit conduit normal.

In fact, I really do not know how *normal* being pursued by a faceless man and his demon steed really is!

"You say that you sensed her?" Doctor Francis asked, breaking my temporary internal mental tirade.

"Yes," I replied. "We mated."

"That bite on your shoulder, did she make it?" asked the doctor.

"Yes. Well the one on the right she did. The one on the left is from that nasty skeleton." I moved my shirt aside so that they could see.

"That is why I was so freaked out by the skeleton biting into Fredrick's head. One almost took my shoulder off!"

This was the first time I had actually looked at it since it happened. The bite was disgusting, and turning a black color because it was so caked with dried blood."

"Then you are only partially mated. A second ritual must occur during a full moon for you and Katherine to be truly mates. You may or may not become werewolf yourself, and in this world, I cannot begin to know if we will ever see a full moon, as it seems we are in a state of perpetual twilight. You will know, however, if the Change takes hold and hopefully, we will be there to help you through it."

"Most humans do not survive the Change," commented Fredrick, "but if you do, you will become werewolf – like us. You can mate Katherine again as wolf and your marriage of flesh and beast will be consummated."

"And your powers heightened," added Doctor Francis.

"Yes," said Fredrick, "Katherine is a very strong wolf. You will share her strength, her talents, just as she will share yours."

CHAPTER 13

My head felt light and I had to sit down. I have signed up for a lot of things in my time, from that stint in the army to who knows how many magazine subscriptions. But this?

Let's see here, I somehow wound up in hell, lost my friend, fucked a werewolf and might possibly become one myself... *IF* the Change doesn't kill me first... or I don't happen to get murdered by some demonic undead being. Just fucking lovely!

Dr. Francis stooped down next to me, "Are you okay?" he asked.

"I don't know," I replied, "all of this is turning my world upside down."

"Tell me about it," Fredrick replied, still eyeing the corpse steed. At least you didn't have some alligator try to crack you in the skull *with* a skull!"

That got a chuckle from the group and I regained some of my composure. *Only a clear head will get you out of this mess, if there's a way out.*

Dr. Francis continued, "We need to find Katherine and regroup as a pack. From here on out, we must stay together. We need you to help us find her."

"I'll do what I can," I said, "but I'm not really sure how accurate my "sixth sense" of her is."

"It will get better over time, but for now do your best. I believe time is running short and regardless, we need to get off this volcano."

He did have a point and I almost forgot about our present situation. Just beyond the corpse steed, lava oozed out from the volcano and covered the area, again reminding me of the lake of fire, as the conquistador so accurately described it. Getting off this thing was going to be tricky. *I wonder how Katherine did it?* I thought.

As if answering my question, Dr. Francis declared, "This way," and began to scale down the mountain from our present position and toward the lava flow. "The lava will gradually work its way downhill. We will follow along its edges and make our way westward toward Leng."

Fredrick followed Dr. Francis' lead. As we were descending he turned to me and said, "Please stay close behind us. We will move very fast. Katherine should sense you as we get closer. Hopefully, she will come back at that point."

It was very hot by the lava and at times, I almost couldn't stand it. Dr. Francis' brisk pace left me little time to worry about the heat, as it took everything I had just to keep up. Now the old doctor no longer looked frail as I stereotyped him earlier, but fit and aggressive. *There is more to this old codger than meets the eye.*

We trekked downward until the lava pooled into a sulfuric lake near the base of the mountain. Our team continued walking along the lake's edge until the terrain began to ascend once more.

To my relief, going up the hill did finally took us away from the lava flow and the temperature cooled a bit.

The air – although still thin – was also more breathable, as there was less ash. It would seem that we had finally moved away from the volcano's fury.

We came to a large clearing that stretched beyond the horizon. Somewhere in the far distance, I could make out the outline of a village of some sort.

"Amazing!" Fredrick exclaimed. "The Village of Leng, as it once was!"

"This is a very historic find!" Dr. Francis said. "I wonder if Katherine went inside or observed from a distance."

As we pondered the circumstance, Fredrick proposed we rest at our present location before journeying to the town. After our grueling pace escaping the volcano, I couldn't agree more.

We didn't have anything to make a true camp with, like tents, food, etc., but we each took turns watching for trouble, while the others rested.

Time had no meaning in this creepy world as there was no difference between night and day. At some point, Katherine emerged.

My heart raced as I saw her approach.

She ran with utmost swiftness across the great plain, like a brown buffalo, but as she drew closer, you could tell she was a very large wolf, or werewolf to be more precise.

Dr. Francis, who had been resting at the time, stood to greet her.

Before our eyes, she changed back into human form. The change looked painful and when it was over, she lay on the earth, covered with sweat and panting.

"The goats were tasty!" she said between breaths.

She grinned and looked at me, "But not worth the trip to get them."

We all had a small laugh at her attempt at humor. After giving her a few moments to rest herself, we brought each other up to speed.

I briefly wondered if she had eaten the nomads as well. I remembered too late that she could read my mind. I got a look that seemed to say, "Wouldn't you like to know." I would not, actually, I thought at her. I was still not sure if she could hear me.

Katherine advised that the town was inhabited with humanoid creatures that resembled dwarfs, but were not lifelike. "They looked like they were undead," she described.

"It is possible that we are seeing an afterlife representation of how the town existed in olden days," Dr. Francis offered.

"But you said the goats were tasty," I proposed.

"Yes, I did eat one," Katherine offered, grinning sheepishly. "I was in wolf form, thus the meal was not memorable. I will say that it didn't seem too filling, as I am very hungry right now."

"The Change also requires a lot of strength," Fredrick said. "I am always hungry when I become wolf and go back to human form."

"There was something of note, Dr. Francis," Katherine said.

"What was that?" he asked.

"I saw a Huaca de la Luna, in the center of the village," she replied.

"A Temple of the Moon?" Dr. Francis said. "Very interesting."

"That's not all," Katherine replied. "The temple was a pyramid and it was glowing!"

Fredrick Gonzalez must have seen the bewilderment on my face because he turned to me and gave me a history lesson, "In a prior archaeological find, remains of a tribe were found in this region. This society lived ages ago and if memory serves me correct, dozens of skeletons were buried together near a sacrificial plaza.

"Defeated warriors often were among those offered at Huaca de la Luna, or the Temple of the Moon."

"That's only part of the story," Dr. Francis said. "Some Nachaie warriors faced sacrifice, too. Whether done to control enemies or please the gods, the Nachaie practiced human sacrifice for over 300 years."

He turned back to Katherine, "You said that the temple glowed. Please describe it."

"The rocks themselves glowed," Katherine said. "It was not like a reflective light, but rather as if light itself was coming from the pyramid. The light was white and faint. Sort of like moonlight."

"Hence the name, 'Temple of the Moon,'" I added.

The three nodded in agreement.

Far off in the distance, a winged horse could be seen. *The corpse steed,* I thought. *It's following us.*

I decided now was as good a time as any to relay the story of Nyarlathotep to Katherine, including his interest in her.

She listened intently; all the while the corpse steed circled our camp like an ominous omen of dark things to come. *It's getting closer. Slowly but surely, it's getting closer.*

"It all makes sense in a strange way," Fredrick said. "Nyarlathotep wants a sacrifice and the Temple of the Moon is glowing. That means that it's in an active state. Perhaps our passageway back to our reality lies in the Temple!"

"You may be correct, Fredrick," Dr. Francis said. "However, we cannot know for certain without going to the temple."

The corpse steed, which had been flying over a kilometer away, suddenly landed and began to walk toward us. With each step, smoke plumed from the ground below its hand-like hoofs. It snorted and even from the distance it could be heard.

"Nyarlathotep is coming for you!" I told Katherine. "We must run, fight, or go to him." I looked at her with utmost sincerity, "I'm not loosing you without a fight."

"Don't worry, my dear," Katherine replied. "I'm not going down without a fight."

"The decision has been made!" Dr. Francis said with a commanding voice. "We change into wolf form and take down the corpse steed!"

He turned directly to me and said, "Stay put! It's going to get bloody."

Fredrick ran up to me, handed me his ruby and said, "Here, in case I don't make it." He grinned in a sad sort of way. "Who knows, it may be worth something someday."

With that, the three of them began to change into werewolves. I watched in amazement as Fredrick's neck wound distorted as joints were pulled out of place and realigned. As he changed, the wound healed. *Amazing,* I thought.

I briefly wondered if Ziggy was a werewolf and if that was why I thought he was healing before I killed him. What an awful thought!

That's just great, Katherine knows now – she is staring at me through those gorgeous eyes.

Her look was confused like she couldn't make out exactly what I was thinking as she got ready to change.

Dr. Francis was a large black werewolf and Fredrick was a large white werewolf with a black stripe in his coat. Dr. Francis' wolf reminded me of a cross between a pit bull, a St. Bernard, and a black bear! Dr. Francis was very large in wolf form. Frederick reminded me of a Siberian husky.

Katherine began changing again and this time, I could tell it was very painful for her. *Too much running, too many changes, too soon. Be careful, it's taking a toll on you,* I thought. She still looked lovely and I found myself growing more and more attracted to her as I watched her change into that golden beast.

Each took off without hesitation and charged toward the corpse steed, which was less than half the distance from where it had landed.

I found a nearby rock and sat down to watch the cosmic battle take place. As I did, Yurak appeared, wagging his tail. He yelped and sat close to me.

The corpse steed – a ghastly creature just to gaze upon – was even more frightful as it took an attack posture. Flames flashed from its nostrils and its razor-sharp teeth glistened a full array of fangs as it met the charge of the three werewolves.

The corpse steed stood up on its hind legs and spread its bat-like wings. The werewolves – though very large creatures by themselves – looked tiny in comparison.

"It has come to this, I see." I spun around to see Nyarlathotep sitting on a rock beside me.

"What do you mean?" I asked.

"All I wanted was for you to bring me your wolf as a pet, now the entire pack of them will die at the hands of my steed," Nyarlathotep said.

"I personally could not sacrifice Katherine," I replied. "Plus, she – they – will not go down without a fight."

"Very well," Nyarlathotep said, settling in to watch the show. "It looks like we'll be entertained this evening."

105

I watched in horror as the white wolf, Fredrick, arrived at the scene first. He ran and lunged at the corpse steed, biting deep into its right bat wing. The corpse steed hissed and returned the blow, biting Fredrick in the nape of his neck.

The powerful jaws of the corpse steed took Fredrick's entire neck in its mouth. It raised the wolf far above its head and crushed its neck. We could hear the snap even from our vantage point. The wolf went limp as the corpse steed threw down its lifeless body in front of the other two attackers.

Dr. Francis changed his attack pattern, going around to the rear of the corpse steed. Katherine followed on the opposite side.

As the corpse steed spun around to follow Dr. Francis, Katherine drove a fierce bite at the corpse steed's left rear leg. The creature bellowed in pain. Katherine began biting and tearing at the wound.

In a grand display, Dr. Francis lunged high and landed on the corpse steed's back. Similar to what the steed did to Fredrick, Dr. Francis bit the corpse steed's neck.

The creature howled again, this time spreading its wings and taking to the air. It had gotten about five feet off the ground when its left rear leg was ripped asunder. The injuries that Katherine administered tore enough of the bone and muscle tissue away that the limb hung loosely. That combined with her hanging from the injured limb was just enough to send both she and the leg falling to the earth.

The corpse steed screamed and bucked toward the sky. Dr. Francis was still hanging on and biting with even more ferociousness.

The beast made it about fifty feet into the air when the earlier injury that Fredrick inflicted on its right wing caused it to free fall straight down. It spun on its back and landed hard on the earth, killing both itself and Dr. Francis instantly.

Katherine lay on the ground near the fallen beings. She was injured slightly from her earlier fall.

Nyarlathotep looked at me. I summoned all my courage and stared into his face, trying to make out anything. All I could see was darkness behind his black cloak. "Your wolf is victorious. I am impressed."

He reached out a boney hand and held out a golden dagger. It was highly ornate and encrusted with emeralds, rubies, and unknown other jewels. "You will need this," he said.

"What for?" I asked, looking at the dagger suspiciously.

"It is your way back," Nyarlathotep replied. "Go at once to the Temple. In the topmost chamber is a ceremonial slab. Make your offering and go home."

As I took the hilt of the dagger, he vanished, leaving me alone with my thoughts. Throughout this exchange, Yurak did not say a word.

I stood up, slid the dagger between my belt and right hip pocket, and jogged across the field to Katherine, the corpse steed, and the rest of our party. Yurak followed me a few paces behind.

The three wolves had changed back to their human form. Dr. Francis and Fredrick Gonzalez had succumbed to their injuries. The corpse steed was lying in a misshapen heap, also dead. Bluish gore and pus oozed from its open wounds. As I slowly moved closer, the steed reeked of a terrible pungent odor.

"Katherine!" I called out. "Are you okay?"

"Uh, not sure," she replied. *At least she is conscious.* "I don't think I broke any bones."

She pulled her nude body up off the ground and turned to look at the dead corpse steed. "What the hell was that?"

"We called it a corpse steed because it resembled both a corpse and a horse," I said and then added, "Corpse horse was harder to pronounce."

"That thing is awful!" Katherine exclaimed.

"Yes," I confirmed. "Let's get away from the stink."

Katherine was not too steady on her feet and I carried her until I was too tired to continue. I placed her gently down on the ground and for a while, we discussed what had just occurred.

"We have to go to the temple," she finally said.

"Yes," I concurred, looking at the dagger.

"I'm not sure what we'll encounter once we get there," Katherine said. She reached out and took my hand. "But whatever happens, we're in this together."

I smiled my best smile and brought her hand to my lips. "Too bad we didn't meet under different circumstances," I said.

She smiled a sad smile and replied, "Well at least you get to go to Leng with your clothes on!"

"I'd offer you the shirt on my back, but I'm not sure you'd want this nasty thing." It was dirty, blood-stained, and reeked of body odor.

She grinned, shaking her head no to decline my offer.

Joking at a time like this, I thought. Had we grown so used to death that we were not even going to acknowledge our losses? Maybe not talking about it would help it go away. *Not so*, I thought, *this would never go away*. Oh well, we must press forward.

CHAPTER 14

We walked slowly toward Leng and talked about our experiences as we went. I completely expected the townsfolk to be adversarial, as everything we had encountered up to this point had been. However as we drew closer, they simply ignored us as if we did not exist.

Perhaps you don't exist to them, I thought.

The village of Leng was similar to Pabilito's with the exception that these people were herdsmen and there were several animal pens and barns. The buildings in this area, thankfully, were in better shape than near the Passageway. Dr. Francis was probably right – this likely was a representation of how life was for these people back when they were alive.

The only thing that seemed out of place in the tiny farming village was the pyramid. It stood in the center of town and as Katherine described earlier, it glowed a faint white light. There were steep stairs that ascended on each of the pyramid's sides and instead of a point being at the top, this pyramid was flat on the top. Each stairway ended in a singular opening just before the top of the pyramid.

Throughout this time, Yurak had never left our side since appearing at the corpse steed battle and even as we carefully climbed the stairs, he climbed with us.

There must have been two hundred stairs or more. It seemed like we climbed forever. The Led Zeppelin song *Stairway To Heaven* came to mind as we finally approached the upper chamber of the structure.

When we walked inside, the dagger began to glow.

On the wall was a fresco with an image of a man with a wolf's head. The being was wearing a strange necklace with a medallion. The medallion was a twelve pointed star with an inverted symbol that was something between the Egyptian ankh and a Christian crucifix. In the dim light, I could not tell for certain.

As Nyarlathotep had promised, a stone slab lay in the center of the room.

As she and I stared at the slab, I turned to Katherine and handed her the dagger. "Sacrifice me and return home."

"I can't," she replied.

"A sacrifice must be made! That is the way of things." The voice came from Nyarlathotep, who had reappeared in the chamber.

"Kill the wolf or kill the man, it is very simple!" Nyarlathotep exclaimed. "But do it now, as my patience wanes."

I moved away from Katherine and laid myself on the cold stone. "Please Katherine, do it and save yourself."

She stood over me and raised the dagger high above my chest. I closed my eyes and waited to feel the blade plunge into my heart.

Unbeknownst to me, Yurak had materialized into a real dog within the confines of the chamber. A split second before bringing the dagger down, she grabbed the dog with blinding speed, put him on the stone slab beside me and drove the dagger into his heart.

I opened my eyes just in time to see his white fur matted with blood. He let out a small yelp, but that was all.

Suddenly the room began to spin and my vision became dark. I was getting very dizzy and about to faint...

CHAPTER 15

"I think he's coming around." Voice One said above my head.

"Here, let's try this," replied Voice Two.

I inhaled a strong aroma of ammonia and began to cough. I opened my eyes and found myself in a hospital bed. Two unknown medical professionals stood beside me and Katherine stood next to them. She was fully clothed in jeans and a tank top. It even looked as if she was wearing makeup.

"What? Where am I?" I asked, completely disoriented.

"There, there," replied Voice One. "Doctor Chavez gave you some medicine to help you wake up. You have been in a coma for almost a week."

"What? A coma?" I replied, bewildered.

"You were with an archeological team," Voice Two said. He had just thrown the ammonia packet into a nearby trashcan. "There was an earthquake and all were killed except you and Miss Katherine." She stroked my arm.

"A white dog led rescue teams into the cave where the team was trapped," Dr. Chavez said. "Only you and the young lady made it out. The dog dug deep into the rubble and found you. Because of him, you were rescued, but he died of exhaustion."

I frowned. This was all too much to take.

Dr. Chavez continued. "We need to keep you in the hospital for a couple more days, but after that you are free to go."

"Where exactly am I?" I asked.

"You are in La Paz," Dr. Chavez replied.

I sat up from my hospital bed and looked around. Sure enough, it looked like I was in a hospital. Had it all been just a terrible dream?

In a way, I was very relieved to be alive and that the horrors I experienced were not real but some strange assembly of thoughts my comatose brain processed to keep me alive while my body healed. I breathed a sigh of relief.

The medical staff started to leave the room. Dr. Chavez paused for a moment and said, "Nurse Alceria will be in to bring you your belongings."

Katherine walked over to a window and looked out onto the day as the nurse came in. She carried a cardboard box and sat it down next to my bed. "Be careful," Nurse Alceria said, "don't let anyone know you have this or they'll take it."

Inside the box was the conquistador's diary. Someone had wrapped it in a knitted fabric pouch that reminded me of a protective sheath that a child might use to protect his schoolbook. I smiled at the precious find that made it back from the journey.

Below it was the broken camera. I had later developed the film, but only three pictures developed and those came out black and white and grainy. My blue jeans were crumpled up in the bottom of the box and looked very dirty. I checked for my wallet, which was still there and noticed something in the left pocket.

The object felt hard, like a rock and when I pulled it out, I almost fainted again.

In the palm of my hand, I held Fredrick's ruby.

PART II: THE CHANGING

CHAPTER 16

For the next three days, Katherine and I did not speak of anything other than the fact that we had been rescued from a cave. *That was logical, wasn't it? We didn't really survive a supernatural phenomenon. Let's proceed under the assumption that nothing happened other than a group of people had the misfortune of being underground during a cave-in. That's all it was, nothing more.*

Katherine seemed to sense my thoughts during our taxi ride to the airport. She reached out and took my hand in hers and smiled sweetly. "Something's bothering you," she said.

"Yes, I suppose." I replied. I was still bandaged up and my shoulder hurt like hell. The doctor's released me, stating that I was scuffed up pretty bad from the rocks and debris.

Katherine agreed to accompany me back to West Virginia, as the doctor insisted that I not travel alone. She had proven herself to be quite an attentive caregiver, which was lovely considering that we had only known each other for a few hours before going into the cavern.

"You can tell me, you know," she said.

"I am not sure I can," I replied.

"Do you think you are going crazy?" she asked.

"Well," I replied. "Dr. Chavez said I was in a coma, but during that time I had the strangest dream. It seemed so real."

Her face, which was smiling, grew pale. "Shit."

"What?" I asked.

"I thought it was just me," she replied. "But, I dreamed we were in a different world. That somehow we had died and went to hell. I dreamed that the devil wanted me as a sacrifice to pay your way back, but you volunteered yourself for me."

I interrupted her story, "And as I was on the slab, you sacrificed Yurak – the camp dog – and we woke up!"

"Yes!" she exclaimed.

"Then it wasn't a dream, was it?" I asked.

"No," she replied. "We both had the experience, but no one would ever believe it, it's too crazy."

"If what happened in the passageway really happened, does that mean we're married?" I asked.

She blushed, "I guess it does. But we're not legally recognized as husband and wife. So I suppose you could still back out after you heal up."

"That's what you get for waking up in Vegas," I said, playing off the words of a Katy Perry song.

"Well," she countered. "That's what you get for mating a she-wolf."

My blood ran cold. The dull ache in my shoulder thudded acutely. "Holy shit!" I exclaimed. "Does that mean..."

"Yes," Katherine replied. "The werewolf part was real. I am one in real life and no one knows. That is, until now."

"So, does that mean I will become one?" I asked.

"Only time will tell," she replied.

"In that case," I said, "I'm glad you're heading back to West Virginia with me."

"Me too," she said.

We French kissed for the next couple minutes until we were interrupted by the taxi driver uttering something in Spanish indicating that we were at the airport.

As damaged as I was psychologically, my story, would have still ended on a high note had we both went to West Virginia and lived happily ever after. That would have been nice.

However, neither Katherine nor I could have expected her visa to be rejected upon entry into the States. As soon as we stepped off the plane, authorities pulled us aside and instructed Katherine to return home, which was in Spain.

"I will be in touch," she said as she was led away.

"Please," I begged the authorities, "isn't there anything we can do?"

But my pleas were ignored as I saw her disappear into their office.

I am not sure why she was detained and as I make this entry, am not sure if I will ever see her again. But I do hope so.

Driving home, I thought about the experience in South America and by the time I arrived at my cabin in the woods near Clarksburg, West Virginia, I had convinced myself that everything I had seen – all that I had witnessed – was make-believe.

I forced myself to believe that I had hallucinated the entire ordeal in the cave and that I was lucky to be alive. Perhaps, I had even hallucinated Katherine and that she was some sort of ghost. Would I see her again? Who knows?

I was glad to be back home and looked forward to settling back into my routine. I didn't even unpack my travel suitcase, but rather left it just inside my front door to get to later.

Walking into my living room, I saw the unfinished chess game still standing on the coffee table. Thoughts of playing chess with Doug before we decided to go on our trip came rushing back to me like blood gushing from an open wound.

You didn't just imagine it, Doug is still dead, my mind protested, but I just ignored it. *Got to get my head out of my ass,* I thought.

The weather was getting colder, but nevertheless, I was determined to sit on my front porch, read the paper, and enjoy a Romeo Y Julieta cigar.

Picking up the paper, I read of a disturbing trend of strange occurrences in the nearby small town of Melas. Police were looking for an explanation as to why people were disappearing. I shook my head and tossed the paper aside. My cozy home just didn't feel as cozy anymore.

In the front yard, a buck deer came out, looked around suspiciously, and darted off into some overgrowth nearby. This time of year, a lot of deer were out and about.

As evening approached, I could see that it was going to be a cold night, with stars piercing the sky and what looked to be a full moon coming out just over the horizon.

I was so tired and jet lagged from the trip that I leaned my head back and passed out there on the porch.

I had the strangest dream: I felt like I was running through the woods. It was a forest I had never been in before. I heard a heavy breathing that was not my own. I experienced sensations that I had never felt before.

I was moving at a very fast pace, keeping to the ground as I went. Everything seemed amplified, my sight and hearing honed sharper then I could remember, but most stunning, my sense of smell was incredible. I could make out something on the ground in the distance. Oddly, it was my nose that 'saw' it, if that makes sense. I quickly approached it, and then faded back to darkness.

When I awoke, I was several hundred yards from my residence. I was lying on damp ground. My clothes were torn and I was covered in a wet, matted substance. My shirt was ripped and my entire body ached. *I must have sleepwalked!*

A deer carcass was lying nearby – the buck I had seen earlier. Its guts were torn from its body and it looked as if it had been attacked by a bear or some other wild animal.

What the hell!? I thought as I looked around, bewildered.

The first rays of dawn's early light were shining through and frost had covered the ground. I was extremely cold. *Fool, you must have been out here all night!*

I pulled myself up from the ground and started my way back to the cabin. I walked into the bathroom and almost screamed. I too looked as though I had been attacked by a wild animal, as I was covered in blood and dirt.

My hands were dirty, bloody, and sore and somehow during the night I had lost my shoes.

I wasn't sure if I had been injured, but it felt like I must have been. My entire body ached. My joints and muscles were very sore, as if I had been exercising and over-exerting myself.

I got into a hot shower and stayed there until the water went cold. Coming out, I looked once more upon the mirror, which had fogged up from the steam.

Using a hair dryer, I cleared off the fog in the mirror, and to my astonishment, my shoulder was completely healed! No sign of a scar could be seen except a small blemish on the skin.

I went through the rest of the day in a haze. I was so exhausted. I felt as if I had been in some kind of wreck or coming down with the flu.

As evening approached, I lied in bed and before long, I was deep in sleep.

That night, I had another dream. Only this time, it was a nightmare and I was back in the passageway. This was the first time I dreamed of that god-awful place since I came back to the States.

I dreamed that I was being chased down a long chiseled corridor. Triangles glistened along the walls and ceiling. Behind me were several snakes and a zombie-apparition of Ziggy in pursuit.

Ziggy screamed out after me, "You didn't kill me soon enough!"

I ran faster. The faster I ran, the longer the tunnel became. I knew if I turned around, the snakes and Ziggy would be upon me.

Suddenly Nyarlathotep stepped out in front of me. I plowed into him, but he did not budge when we collided. He grabbed my upper arms with death-like strength.

"Let go of me!" I yelled.

"You thought you were clever. You and your wolf!" Nyarlathotep hissed. "You should have sacrificed her on the slab when you had the chance!"

I struggled but could not break free from his grasp.

"You cannot save her, you know," Nyarlathotep said, his voice becoming very calm.

"What are you talking about?" I asked.

"Augustine knows you made it back," Nyarlathotep jeered.

"I don't know anyone named Augustine!" I replied.

"That makes no difference," Nyarlathotep countered. "He found out about your wolf visiting the undead worlds and returning. He dreams too!"

"What?" I asked, very much confused.

Nyarlathotep continued: "Augustine is the Master Wolf. I created him. He created your wolf."

I felt myself beginning to stir from the nightmare. It was the next day.

CHAPTER 17

A full week went by before I received the call. A frantic Katherine was on the other end of the receiver.

"It's me. You've got to help!"

"Katherine? Is that you? Please calm down. What's wrong?" I asked.

"I don't know where to begin," she started. There were obvious tears in her voice.

"I'm calling you from Madrid. After they detained me, I was deported to Spain. They got me on an expired visa."

"That doesn't sound too bad," I replied. "We can fix that over time, I'm sure."

"That's not the problem," Katherine said. "A week ago, during the full moon, I experienced the Change."

A lump formed in my throat. I could barely speak. "Go on."

"When I came back to my flat, there were two dead bodies."

"Did you..." I started to say.

Katherine interrupted, "No. I didn't kill them. They were complete strangers. Both were shot. The police found a pistol with my fingerprints on it and charged me with a double murder."

"Holy crap!" I exclaimed. "What happened?"

"That's the problem – I don't know! Whenever the Change occurs, I go far away to a wooded area away from population – hunt things like rabbits and stuff – and return when it is over. I am in control, believe me!" She began weeping.

"I believe you Katherine." I tried to sound soothing and added the next part carefully. "How did those people wind up at your place?"

"I don't know!" she exclaimed between sobs. "The pistol they found was a .357 magnum that I bought twenty years ago. I kept it in a drawer for protection. I haven't shot it much at all since then. It was a man and a woman."

"So, the police think you killed this couple?"

"That's what I'm telling you! They were killed with MY .357 magnum handgun! But I didn't do it! I told you I was out on my own hunt in the woods, but have no alibi. I was framed!"

"This is bad news, Katherine," I said sincerely.

"Please come. I really need you here."

I looked across my living room at the unpacked travel suitcase standing ready for deployment. *Katherine needs me*, I thought. "I'm on my way."

Five hours later, I was on a plane to Madrid, Spain. I had never been to Spain before and honestly did not know where to begin or even how to help Katherine. Hell, I didn't even speak Spanish all that well!

After boarding, I settled in for a long trip. The duration of the flight from New York to Madrid was to be a little over seven hours. As the jet took to the night, I closed my eyes in hopes that I could get some shuteye.

At some point, I dozed off and dreamed that I was back in the Temple of the Moon. Katherine was standing beside me.

"You're here," she said

"This is a dream," I replied.

"We're still bonded," Katherine said in return.

"Why are we back here?" I asked.

"For several nights, the amulet has haunted at my conscious."

"What amulet are you talking about?" I asked.

"The one on the fresco."

We both looked up and saw the image of the wolfman and the strange necklace he was wearing.

"I had forgotten about this detail," I said. "Everything happened so quickly. Most of what happened in the temple left my mind when I woke up in the hospital. I even told myself that it was all a bizarre chemical imbalance or something that I experienced. In other words, I am in denial."

"You did not make it up, honey," she said softly. "I was there. As bad as it was, it was indeed real."

"But this dream isn't real, is it?" I protested.

"I am with you in spirit," she said. She took me by the hand and turned me to face her. "We are linked, remember?"

"Yes. How can I forget?" I replied.

"Right now, I am physically in a cold Madrid jail cell. My attorney is named Max Donetello. He will see you when you arrive."

She turned back to face the fresco.

"What is it about this picture that bothers you so?" I asked.

"I don't know, there's something about it," she replied.

Just then, the plane experienced some turbulence and I was jarred awake. I spent the next two hours trying to return to sleep, but it remained elusive. I did have the frame of mind to write down the name she gave me in the dream and make it a point to look up the attorney once I had settled in.

I also took the time to draw the amulet the best I could remember so that I could discuss it further with Katherine once I saw her in person.

I was completely beat when the plane touched down at the Madrid-Barajas Airport. Apprehensively I trudged through what seemed like an excessively long terminal.

When I finally made it to baggage claim, a short Spanish gentleman with dark hair and beard stood with a sign bearing my name.

I met him and was relieved that he spoke English. He introduced himself as Max Donetello. A limousine was waiting nearby and he motioned me inside.

"A friend of Katherine's is a friend of mine," Max said as we got underway. "I have booked a room for you at a nearby Hilton."

"Thank you, Mr. Donetello," I replied.

"We don't have a lot of time, as you know," Max continued. "In just over twenty-two days, Katherine will change into a werewolf and the authorities will be forced to kill her."

"So you know about Katherine's gift?" I asked.

"Yes," Max replied. "It's more like a curse if you ask me – especially this time. We are a secret society." Max looked gravely at me. "And we must continue to keep it secret, as I am sure you can imagine."

I nodded. Max continued, "Most of the pack was with her on the expedition. I stayed here, as I am not an explorer. I am the pack's attorney. I keep their finances and legal matters in check."

"Katherine said she was framed for a double murder," I said. "Do you have any additional information that we can use to get her out?"

He shook his head in disgust. "I was in Barcelona when it happened. The authorities paged me to come right away.

"I wish I had some kind of information that could be of use," Max continued. "It is just that all of this happened so quickly. It has only been a week since they hauled her off to jail. I worked my ass off trying to get her out on bail, but they won't budge. They think they have a rock-solid case."

"So, how do you know Katherine?" I asked. Secretly, I hoped to gauge this person's sincerity to help Katherine.

"In addition to knowing her through pack business, Katherine comes over to the house to tutor my daughter in language studies – when she's not out of the country, of course.

"She is an excellent communicator. My wife Tiana just adores Katherine's ability to communicate with our little girl. She is a very gifted linguist."

I nodded, "I figured that much from my brief time in South America with her."

"She told me at the jail that you are her fiancé," Max said. "I hope to get to know you."

I felt nervous at his remark, but remained neutral. Things were happening so quickly. "We have a spiritual bond."

Max nodded in an understanding way. "You have mated then? Have you experienced the Change?"

"I don't really know," I replied. That was the truth. *What the heck do you know any more?* My inner voice taunted at my conscious.

Max looked sternly at me, "You don't know? How can that be?"

I sunk back in the black leather seats of the limo. "I really don't know, Max. I had just gotten back to my house when the full moon hit. I remember sleeping on my porch and I woke up the next morning in my yard."

Max looked confused. "The Change is very painful. In fact, most who experience it for the first time succumb to the event and don't survive. Cardiac arrest." He squinted at me and said, "If you had changed, you would know it."

I thought about how I had sleepwalked in my local forest and of the dead deer that I had found that day, but decided that I did not know Max well enough to start speculating. My sanity was frail enough as it was.

I thought it wise to change the subject. "Do you know what the victims were doing before they came to Katherine's house?"

"No," Max replied. "That has not yet been determined."

"Perhaps there was something in their pockets or in a purse. Cell phone records, perhaps?" I asked.

"Very wise," Max concurred. "I will check with the authorities to see if I can have a look at what they took from the scene. In any case, we will need it for a good defense."

"I am hoping that will turn up a lead. If we can determine where they were before they arrived at her place, then we may be able to find someone else who knows something."

"I'll get working on that," said Max. "Meanwhile, you get some rest and I'll call you in the morning."

Although I did rest to some extent on the airplane, Max had a point. After the limo pulled away, I checked in to the hotel and made my way up to the room.

As I opened up my suitcase, I noticed that the conquistador's diary was still in the knitted pouch, just like I left it when I left Peru.

I took it out to examine it once more. I saw there were only a few pages remaining to be read, so I decided to read them before resting in hopes that the art of translation would help me to fall asleep faster.

We emerged into some unknown desert region. In our hasty retreat, we must have took a wrong turn and came out on the other side of the mountain.

I dare say that I am most confused. My men and I have thoroughly scouted around this region and I have not seen this territory before. I know that we did not travel too far to be at a point of such unfamiliarity - even our most seasoned scouts are baffled by this.

The best I can describe this place is that we are in a desert. It is quite barren and as far as I can tell, there is no vegetation. It is a stark contrast to where we entered. A long ways off is a village. We will make our way there and attempt to obtain some answers.

27 September 1530

We have hiked for three days and the men have started to complain. Something is unreal about this place. Although I can attest that we have indeed traveled for three days, nightfall has never set in the sky. It is always in a state between late afternoon and early evening.

Our food and rations are about to run out. We will be at the village soon and hope to acquire supplies.

PASSAGEWAY

The village is some kind of trap! It is a city of ghosts! The men were most frightened. It is an unholy place!

When we arrived, we noticed that it resembled the village Leng that we raided earlier in the month. The oddity was that the structures that we burnt were still standing and in this version of the town, there was a large pyramid marked with the triangular patterns that were carved on the cave walls!

As we approached the pyramid, the villagers began to attack us. They were indeed ghosts, as some were transparent. However, when they struck, their blows could be felt!

Rather than fight such an abomination, we fled back towards the mountain.

The ghosts ceased their pursuit as soon as we cleared the first ridge beyond the village. As we marched briskly back, the earth itself began to shake and red molten rock began to flow from its depts. I have never seen anything like this before in my entire life.

This red ooze began to fill the next valley that we had to cross in order to make it back to the cave. This is surely the work of the devil, of that I have no doubt.

Journal update:

Two of my finest men – Javier and Armundo – were swallowed by the earth itself as we tried to make it across the lake of fire.

I say lake of fire because the red ooze has filled most of the valley, making a hasty crossing impossible. The morale of my troops is starting to shatter. Only Christopher, Fernando, and myself remain.

We were able to make it across the lake to the next ridge. To my best estimate, we should be back at the cave within a few hours. We will rest for a while here before continuing.

28 September 1530

It has been one day since my last entry and I felt it wise to carefully record what I saw in the event that I don't make it out of here alive.

I am back in the cavern, but it is only me. Shortly after taking rest Fernando, who was on watch, was attacked by a very large wolf. In all of my life, I had never seen a wolf that size. Its face was long and menacing.

The wolf was so fast. The beast took our brother Fernando by complete surprise but not before he alerted us who were sleeping off the terror.

The creature looked to be the size of Fernando. He had him pinned to the ground and had bitten Fernando deeply in his chest. It was a mortal wound and Fernando immediately died. I quickly grabbed my sword and struck at the creature. I drove it into his side, but it moved away with uncanny speed.

Christopher grabbed the beast from close range and wrestled it to the ground. Of peculiar note, the wolf was wearing some kind of charm. During the struggle, the charm became dislodged and fell to the ground.

During this brief moment, Christopher was able to overtake the beast. He managed to stab the wolf with his dagger as they wrestled.

To my astonishment and horror, the wolf began to change into a man! My God, what have I witnessed!? I

131

had expected to see Christopher take the advantage of the changing to finish off the creature, but Christopher was not moving.

I rushed to his side to see that he had somehow landed on a sharp rock and had broken his back. I was stunned. The man-wolf took my hesitation to his advantage and lunged for me. He did tackle me, but I was swift to my feet. I certainly expected him to come up with a counter attack but instead he grabbed the charm that had fallen to the ground and ran a few paces in the distance.

I watched as he placed the charm back around his neck and to my complete astonishment, his wounds began to heal before my very eyes! Rather than pursue this unholy apparition, I ran as fast as I could. I made it back to the skull cave where I await.

I don't know what will happen to me, but as I document this, I am fortunate to at least have my life. The walls are starting to shake. I must move deeper into the cave...

CHAPTER 18

I was awakened the next morning by the ringing of the telephone. I apparently dozed off in the recliner that sat next to the bed while I read the conquistador's fantastic and tragic tale.

It was Max's voice on the other end over a noisy connection. "Your suggestion turned up something."

"Max, I can't hear you too well," I replied.

"I need you to come right away to Cafe LeRue," Max urged. "We might be on to something."

"Can you tell me over the phone, Max?" I asked.

"No," he replied. "There are too many ears. We need to speak in private."

A few minutes later, I was in a taxi heading to Cafe LeRue to meet Max.

Cafe LeRue was on Paseo del Prado, a chic section of town filled with shops and buildings of distinctive Spanish design. There were several museums here and if I am able to get Katherine out of her present circumstance, I hope to have her show me around.

Upon entering the cafe itself, I was awestruck. The restaurant was terraced into several rising sections. Each terrace held lush vegetation suspended above the ground. I walked through an arched walkway underneath a terrace with vegetation growing just overhead.

There were stairs leading up to the next terrace with tables arranged tastefully on each level. As one went deeper into the body of the building, these plants provided a natural canopy that made me think of the Hanging Gardens of Babylon. I'm glad Max picked this place.

Near the back of the second rise, Max saw me and motioned me to his table. The place had started to fill up but hadn't gotten too busy yet.

"Nice choice of meeting spots, Max," I said as I shook his hand.

"I'm glad it meets the American's approval," he said with a smile.

"So, whatcha got?" I asked with a little bit of slang.

"According to the medical examiner's report, they placed the time of death about fifteen hours before Katherine returned home." Max pulled out a map of Spain and continued. "This is important, because when the change occurs, she goes to the pack's farm here." He pointed to a remote section of the map with the word "Escopete" on it. It looked to be a good distance from Madrid. "To be more specific, the murders occurred around six o'clock pm."

I was confused. "Please explain," I asked.

"It is pack protocol to be at the farm before dusk during times of a full moon. No one can risk being stuck in traffic or in a populated area. As I told you yesterday, we are a secret society. Too much is at stake should we be discovered."

I nodded and added my thoughts, "So you are saying that there was not enough time for Katherine to commit the murders and then get to the farm before the change happened."

"Exactly!" Max said.

"Which supports our mutual belief that Katherine could not have committed the crime," I said.

"But that's not all," Max said; his voice becoming darker.

I looked inquisitively at him.

He continued, "The report showed traces of silver in the wound zones."

"Silver?"

"Yes," replied Max. "They were shot with silver bullets."

"Which means?"

"Which means, they were most likely werewolves!"

"You have to be kidding me!" I said in disbelief. "You mean to say that they were killed because they were werewolves and they just so happened to be shot at Katherine's house?"

"I haven't pieced it all together yet," Max said. "But it does tighten up the suspect pool from a rogue killing to someone who knew these people and how to kill them."

"So, it is a werewolf hunter? Kind of like a vampire hunter?" I asked.

"A werewolf hunter or another werewolf," Max replied and continued, "With this data, I was able to find out which pack they were in. They were both from Valencia. Their pack leader is Rudolfo Vladimir. He is a Russian immigrant who has a coastal shipping operation. I have taken the liberty of calling him on the matter and he has asked to speak with us."

Max leaned forward and whispered the next part, "Rudolfo is very dangerous. The news was surprising to him. He has pledged vengeance and offers his full cooperation." He looked around to make sure no one was within earshot. "He is connected with certain... people. He may be able to find out who did this and most importantly, find a way to get your Katherine out."

"Looks like we are going to the beach."

"It appears that way."

Upon leaving the restaurant, I could almost smell danger and could hear approaching footsteps. I turned quickly, but did not see anyone. Max seemed to notice it too.

"We may have company," Max said.

Just then two thugs jumped out in front of us. The one on the left pulled out a knife and lunged at Max. Max moved faster than I thought was humanly possible and quickly dodged the blow, returning one of his own. He hit Thug Number One with such force that I could her the man's jawbone shatter as he went sprawling backwards and onto the sidewalk.

Thug Number Two was coming toward me but the sight of his partner being quickly disposed of distracted him enough to allow me to punch him squarely in his solar plexus. The thug was startled and dropped to his knees, gasping for air. I must admit that I was a bit surprised, as I didn't think the punch had THAT much impact, but I had little time to reflect. Max quickly jumped in front of me and kicked Thug Number Two in the head, rendering him unconscious.

"Quick, let's get out of here before authorities show up!" he exclaimed. Together we crossed the busy Paseo del Prado and darted into an alleyway. "The parking garage is this way," Max said.

We moved swiftly through a couple city blocks until we found the parking garage. We walked together to Max's Mercedes. "Get in. We're going to the train station."

As we pulled away in the car, I picked up the obvious conversation that needed to happen. "I can't believe we almost got mugged."

"I don't think it was a mugging attempt," Max replied. "Someone is worried about us."

"What do you mean?" I asked. "Heck, I just arrived in town yesterday and haven't called anyone. You are the only person I have spoken with since I got here."

"That's just it," Max replied. "The only thing I can deduce is that I am being monitored. They know I am trying to get Katherine out of jail and are trying to stop me."

"Well if that's the case," I said, "You handled yourself pretty well."

Max grinned, "Not too bad for an eighty-year-old man, aye?"

"Eighty?" I said with disbelief. "Heck, I thought you were in your forties!"

Max winked. "I've been around for quite some time, son. But I will say this, you noticed them coming even before they showed up – just as I had. Maybe you are kindred."

"Kindred?" I asked.

"One of the cursed ones," Max replied. "Once afflicted with lycanthropy your sense of sight, hearing, and smell are greatly improved over that of an ordinary human." He paused for effect. "You sensed the danger just as I did. We were a few steps ahead of the ambush because we knew they were approaching. Also, I saw how swiftly you struck the other attacker. You leveled him." Max grinned.

Max guided the Mercedes along a series of roadways until we were near the Atocha Train Station. "We're taking the Alaris to Valencia," he said matter-of-factly. Rudolfo will have a car to pick us up when we arrive."

I must admit that experiencing Europe's high-speed rail was exciting. I had not expected to use it today, but things were picking up and we had to go with the flow. Even though it was high speed, our trip still took around three hours and I was relieved when we had finally arrived.

A muscular, bearded man greeted us as we stepped off the train. Max recognized him.

"Demetri," he said, shaking the man's hand. "Good to see you again." He introduced us and we headed out to meet Rudolfo.

Demetri picked us up in a black van and off we sped through the streets of Spain's third largest city. Demetri and Max began speaking in Spanish and, while they were talking, I let my mind wonder and tried to take in the sights around me.

I found that was no easy task. I was becoming quickly disoriented as Demetri guided the van through maze-like streets. His windows were rolled down and I could smell a vast variety of foods coming from all over. Suddenly I realized how hungry I was. *Hungry like a wolf,* my mind suggested.

After a while we made it to a warehouse and shipping district. Sea containers were stacked in endless rows as we passed them. Eventually we arrived at a small utilitarian-style building that looked like a center of operations for this area.

The structure reminded me of an army barracks nestled amongst a city of shipping containers. Inside, similar to the feel of the outside, that everything was efficient and businesslike. That impression quickly changed once we crossed the main office and entered a second chamber.

This section seemed more like a private luxury quarters than a seaside logistics base. It had three overstuffed leather sofas arranged around a coffee table, a wet bar off to the far side of the room, and a flat screen television was mounted to the wall. The television had a series of boxes displaying various security cameras watching the shipping operation.

"Zdravstvuyte Max! I see you have arrived in one piece." The voice came from a clean-shaven man who stood about six feet tall, weighed approximately 200 pounds, and had blonde, crew-cut hair.

"Rudolfo," Max replied. "Thanks for having us on short notice." He looked at me up and down, then shook my hand in greeting.

"Dire times old friend," Rudolfo replied. "We have much to discuss. Please have a seat." He motioned for us to sit down in one of the leather sofas and he brought a bottle of vodka and some glasses and sat them on the coffee table. "How is the princess holding up?"

I looked curiously at Rudolfo after his remark, but did not say anything. I was not sure if he was being sarcastic or if he meant something else.

"All things considered, she's doing okay," Max said. "She's not used to being in jail, you know. And right now they are not letting anyone in to see her."

Rudolfo shook his head and looked agitated. "I believe I know who is behind this. What I don't know is why." He poured us all a shot of vodka and continued. "Max, as you know, Bram and Natasha were part of my pack. In fact, I had sent them to speak with Katherine – to warn her of what I learned."

Max had started to say something, but Rudolfo interrupted. "Before you start with pack protocol bullshit and how I should have contacted the Madrid leader, remember that most of them died down in that South American incident last month and you, I couldn't even reach."

Max nodded, "Yes, I was in Barcelona."

Rudolfo continued, "In any case, I learned of an immediate threat on the princess's life. Even though the full moon was coming, we had to warn her. I sent Bram and Natasha to her residence to tell her what I learned. Fortunately, the princess was not there. Unfortunately, the assassin was. He killed them when they came in to look for her."

He slammed his shot glass on the table. His eyes glowed yellow with a barely suppressed rage. Seeing the wolf eyes for the first time since the experience in the passageway reminded me of Katherine changing into the wolf.

Despite his initial pleasantries, Rudolfo was obviously upset. To me, he appeared to be someone who liked being in control. With two of his crew killed and an innocent 'wolf' in jail – framed for the other two's murder – this situation was obviously out of control. *I just hope to hell he doesn't turn into a wolf right here in the office!* I thought to myself. An enraged Russian werewolf could not be a good thing.

"I have reason to believe that Augustine is behind this," Rudolfo said.

Suddenly my stomach filled with acid and Nyarlathotep's words came flooding to my mind, *Augustine knows you made it back.*

"You mean THE Augustine?" Max asked back at Rudolfo with obvious skepticism in his voice. "He is more of a myth than real. Besides what on earth could he possibly want with Katherine?"

"I'm telling you, he is real and on good authority I know he was in Madrid at the time of the incident."

"No disrespect, Rudolfo," Max carefully said, "but none of us know what he looks like. How do you know he was in Madrid?"

"As you know, Maximilian," Rudolfo said, "I am very well connected with those in the Russian government." He poured each of us more vodka and displayed a folder he had sitting nearby.

The first page he pulled out had a photograph of what looked like an Italian luxury hotel. It was setting on a knoll overlooking a large body of water. "This is a palace in Praskoveevka."

He pulled out another photograph of a black limousine near the front with armed men getting out. "One of these men is Augustine de Marnac."

"But Rudolfo," Max protested. "Augustine is a myth. How are you so sure now?"

"Hold up gentlemen," I said, speaking up for the first time since I arrived. "Please help me understand what you two are talking about."

Max replied first, "It is believed that the werewolf curse was first passed down from a master werewolf. He went by the name Augustine and it was said that he was one of the Roman soldiers that participated in the crucifixion of Christ. Specifically, he was the one who speared him when nailed to the cross."

"Whether that is true or not remains to be seen," Rudolfo interjected.

Max continued, "It is believed that he is the ultimate werewolf and cannot be killed. He is also a lone wolf and is one of the few who doesn't run in packs.

"He has killed hundreds of souls over the centuries as it is his style never to let them live. However from time to time one gets away.

"Eventually, these newly cursed individuals discover they are afflicted with the lycanthropy and either die during the Change or one of the packs finds them and helps them make the adjustment.

"The packs all have a grudge against this Alpha and thus he never reveals himself as a werewolf. When he shows up, people die.

"Rudolfo here has been keeping tabs on several Russian businesses that we collectively call 'Augustine' as we suspect they are werewolf owned, but cannot link them to any specific pack."

Rudolfo jumped in, "There are a series of companies that have been funneling money from the government that we cannot track. And mind you, my reach is pretty extensive." Rudolfo grinned and for a moment his eyes turned to normal, "Let's just say that we usually have a piece of this action.

"However, there are a handful of companies that operate outside of both the government and the back channels. Max can attest that even his attorney skills cannot track down the owners of the Augustine companies."

Max nodded in agreement.

"We have tracked them to some degree," Rudolfo remarked. "At first each company we looked into revealed that it was owned by another company – and so forth and so on. It was maddening. We almost resigned ourselves to thinking that it was just some major conglomerate of companies held by many people.

"However these companies go back hundreds of years. I stopped searching after five hundred years." He stared right at me as if to make a point. "Their roots – as entangled as they are – go very deep. We have learned that one person – someone of vast wealth, cunning, and intelligence – controls all of this. But most importantly, he is someone who does not want us to know he controls all of this."

"So what you are saying," I asked, "is that this Augustine de Marnac is one of the gentlemen in this photo and he is the ultimate alpha wolf who has been around for over 2000 years?"

Rudolfo was just about to answer when all of the sudden, shots rang out in the adjoining office. Several of the men screamed.

We all looked up simultaneously at the television as it displayed the closed-circuit security footage. Three of the workers, including Demetri, were lying on the floor mortally wounded. There was a lone gunman wielding a submachine gun spraying the office.

The gunman paused momentarily to survey the carnage and then proceeded to the office door where we were!

With amazing speed, Rudolfo transformed into a werewolf right before my very eyes! It was awesome and hellishly scary. Max assisted in opening the office door and seconds later he was out and upon the attacker.

The attacker was caught by complete surprise as Rudolfo literally bit the attacker's arm so hard that he ripped it from the socket! Gore and blood shot everywhere. What a sight!

Next, Rudolfo grabbed the gunman by his throat with his mouth and ripped it out.

Max too looked as if he were about to change, but realized that he would not need to since the attacker was dead.

I was stunned and dared not go out. *You didn't just witness that; just get it out of your head. Close your eyes, open them, and everything will be okay.* My self-pacifying did not work, as the scene was just as I saw it and I could not blink it away.

Almost as if to drive a point home, Rudolfo buried his muzzle into the gaping throat wound and ripped at the flesh some more.

To my shock and astonishment, Rudolfo opened his mouth and ate the man's entire neck, snapping the body from the head. *Damn that was gruesome!*

"You stay here in the office until Rudolfo calms down," Max advised.

"No shit," I replied. He didn't need to tell me to stay put.

CHAPTER 19

It took a few days to get the 'shop' operational again. I was surprised at how effectively Rudolfo managed his business and how efficiently the wolf pack took care of incidentals (like disposing of the bodies and keeping authorities at bay).

During the cleanup, I made it a point to ask why a similar courtesy was not extended to Katherine. I was told that with Max being out of town at the time of the incident and her other pack members getting killed in South America, the infrastructure was not there to get her off the hook.

Rudolfo put us up at the Las Arenas Balnerario Hotel while his pack stabilized the home front. Max was given the historical documents to review and we spent the next few days in wait.

Max made some phone calls on his end and did his best to confirm what Rudolfo had said. One of the calls was to Julian Montalba, the lead detective on the case. I was relieved to learn that the two went way back and that Julian had no problems openly discussing Katherine's case with Max. However, I should not have been too surprised, as Max was her defense lawyer and sometimes authorities work with the defense in all fairness.

Julian advised that there was enough evidence to push forward with Katherine's prosecution. Their forensics team did a gun-firing test and determined that Katherine's gun was in fact used to commit the crime.

What Max asked next of Julian made me respect him even more as a clever individual. Max asked if there were any similarities to the bullets themselves used in the crime and that of other crimes. Julian did say that there were a few murders in the former Soviet Union countries that involved silver bullets. Max urged (as a favor to an old friend) Julian to check with Interpol to confirm the information, as Max believed that others were involved.

Julian agreed and we waited for another day.

Sometime the following afternoon, Julian called Max and advised that the casings of the silver bullets carried a unique marking of a sickle with a Cyrillic letter for Z – Ж. Julian advised that the prosecutor could easily argue that Katherine simply bought the bullets from the same Russian who made them and still committed the murders. He closed the call by suggesting that Max find more evidence if he wanted to get Katherine released.

He also said that various parties within Interpol law enforcement were highly interested in who made the bullets. The identity of the craftsman is still a mystery.

We came to a mutual consensus that Rudolfo was telling the truth about his suspicion that one person controlled a large empire within Russia. However, whether this person was involved in Katherine being framed was still up for debate.

We confided amongst ourselves and decided to bring Rudolfo in on what we learned. He didn't seem surprised when we told him about the bullets and brought out a small paper sack. He dumped the casings he collected when cleaning up the office on the table.

"The bullets were made by Zinoviy," Rudolfo said. "That is his signature. For the right price Zinoviy can make just about anything.

147

"I used to cover for him, being that we are in a similar line of work, and call on his services from time to time." Rudolfo continued. "However, not any more! These casings have the same mark as the casings that your detective friend found at Katherine's crime scene. It looks like Zinoviy is working with an enemy to supply werewolf-lethal bullets. Most of my pack are dead because of him. He must be stopped!"

He sternly looked at Max. "We cannot take this to the Spanish authorities, there is not enough evidence."

"Do you know where to find him?" I asked.

"Aye," Rudolfo replied. "He operates from Agriya." He hit his forehead with his right palm. "I should have realized this! Agriya is just a few kilometers from Praskoveevka! Hell, it is just down the street from Augustine's palace!"

He pulled Max off to the side and went over some incidentals that would need to be covered before the next move. Max advised me to rest up for a day or two. Rudolfo would be back. I could only assume that Rudolfo was running something behind the scenes to make our access into these Russian cities discrete and off the books.

Later that night, when I had some down time, I tried to meditate and reach out to Katherine in my thoughts. In a *living dimension*, the telepathic process was not as clear as it had been in the passageway. That alone made me question once again if the link had been real at all.

Then again, from what I had been witnessing this week alone, I should have little doubt in the supernatural.

However, on the evening of the third night, I dreamed once more with Katherine. We were standing next to each other on some unknown shore. It was a calm evening.

Katherine had a look of worry that overshadowed the tranquil atmosphere of the beach we were on.

"I'm having a rough time in jail," she said. "They're keeping me in isolation."

"I wish I could see you," I replied.

"You see me now."

I smiled.

"Remember the amulet?" she asked.

"The one on the wall?"

"Yes," she said. "I have been thinking about it again. Something about it has been bothering me."

"What is it?"

"It all happened so fast," she replied. "The night I was attacked. Plus it was so long ago." She trembled and I held her hand.

Katherine continued, "I never thought much about it at the time, but I think the wolf that attacked me was wearing a necklace like the one on the fresco."

"Do you think they are part of a wolf pack?" I asked.

"I really don't know," she said. "Maybe it's my imagination. Maybe it's my nerves. So much has happened so quickly."

I squeezed her hand and hugged her with my mind.

"Thank you so much for helping me. You and Max mean the world to me," Katherine said.

"Do you know Rudolfo?" I asked.

"Yes," she replied. "We go way back."

"He called you 'princess' when I first saw him," I replied.

"Yes," she said. "Rudolfo still calls me that even after all these years."

"Why?" I asked.

"I guess it is time you should know, especially since you are my mate," Katherine said. The words that followed blew my mind. "I am a direct descendent of Catherine II the Great, Empress of all Russia. She was my great grandmother.

"In the early 1800s, I went to Spain to attend the University. You know what happened while I was there. However, because I had been cursed to live out my life as a werewolf, I could not return to my royal family.

"Some years later, Rudolfo was sent by my father Alexander to determine my whereabouts. Rudolfo was a general under my father.

"Anyway, he found out that I had been attacked in Madrid and was critically wounded. He vowed to find out who did this.

"He searched for weeks in Madrid until he located the werewolf that attacked me. A bloody fight ensued and he too was wounded badly. However, Rudolfo had stabbed the wolf and made him flee before it killed him."

Katherine sighed. A lone tear rolled down her cheek in the dream, "Of course, since Rudolfo survived the attack, he too became a werewolf."

"I am so very sorry," I said.

"Don't be," she said. "We both ultimately survived and made a life for ourselves in Spain. We kept in touch."

As if sensing that I needed to know more she added, "There was never anything romantic between us. Rudolfo was like a big brother to me back in Russia. That is why my father sent him to find me."

We stood in silence holding hands until the dream faded away.

**

Within a week, we had special government-like documents written in Russian. Don't ask me to read what they said, but Rudolfo assured us that we would not need them as long as we traveled in his company.

I was rather surprised, to say the least, when Rudolfo took us to the airport. Waiting there was a Leer jet. We all got in and made the 2000-mile trip across the continent.

A few hours later, in the dead of night, we landed in Krasnodar, Russia.

Rudolfo discretely led us through customs and to a private area of the terminal where a Dartz Pombron was parked. Rudolfo had it specially delivered to the airport for our mission.

I had never seen such a vehicle before that night. It was a sports utility vehicle that was part SUV and part tank! The outside looked impenetrable, but the inside was pure luxury. It didn't take me long to realize that the people I was involved with were exceptionally wealthy and enjoyed top-of-the-line security and luxury.

With great haste, we sped through the night. Sometime before 1:00 a.m., we arrived outside Augustine's luxurious beachfront palace.

"My sources tell me that he is here," Rudolfo affirmed.

I certainly hope so after dragging us halfway around the world, my cynical brain thought, but I said nothing. Actually, I wasn't looking forward to meeting Augustine. I knew in my heart of hearts that nothing would be settled rationally.

In the Pombron's headlights I could make out the silhouette of a large stone lion overlooking an extended driveway leading up to the complex. The palace itself was dark on the outside, which may have been a security feature. This was, after all, a private residence and not a luxury hotel that we were rolling up to.

Halfway up the driveway, a wrought iron fence blocked our way. A guard who looked like he had been sleeping in a nearby shelter suddenly sat upright as he saw the Pombron approach.

Rudolfo began speaking to the guard in Russian. About two seconds later, Rudolfo pulled out a pistol with a silencer on it and shot the guard in the head, killing him instantly. My heart raced and I tried not to reveal my shock.

"Pay no mind," Rudolfo said. "How do you Americans say it, 'It's all par for the course.'" He chuckled but there was no way I could think lightly of what I just witnessed.

Rudolfo got out of the Pombron and with superhuman strength dislodged the gate from its locking mechanism. It let out a mechanical moan in disapproval as he pushed it open.

Rudolfo hurried back to the Pombron and resumed the drive.

Max looked around nervously as we proceeded through the gate, but remained silent. Perhaps he too knew that what we were doing was extremely dangerous, crazy, or both, but knew we were past the point of no return.

As we approached the front door, the sounds of automatic weapons could be heard. Bullets began peppering the Pombron's side, but they did not penetrate it. One, two, three bullets hit the windshield and it too withstood the onslaught of bullets.

"Man they are quick," Rudolfo said as he floored the car in the direction of the gunman. Within seconds, he drove the vehicle through some manicured bushes and into the gunman. The gunman screamed as the Pombron drove over top of him.

"It's how do you say, uh yes, show time!" Rudolfo said, and we knew it was our cue to exit the safe enclave of the Pombron.

The front door had a similar gate as the driveway, but as before, Rudolfo simply pulled it open. As he did, he cried, "Ouch! Damn bars are made of silver!" He clinched his hands as if they had just been burnt.

Once the gate was pulled open, the only thing left was an enormous arched oak door. It was unlocked and opened with ease.

As soon as we entered the foyer, the soft sounds of Johann Strauss II's *Blue Danube Waltz* were coming through a whole-house music system.

In some ways this was a surreal touch to the macabre entrance we just made.

We all rapidly looked around the room for signs of danger. The floor of the palace was polished marble and was the most lavish place I had ever set foot in. A thirty-foot-wide crystal chandelier hung directly over our heads.

Moving carefully, we crossed the foyer and came to a large staircase. Rudolfo turned to me and said, "Wait here. Augustine must be upstairs. Maybe sleeping."

"Hopefully," Max added. The two men quickly went upstairs leaving me alone in the foyer.

Honestly, I was petrified. I didn't know if I would encounter any more guards or if my two new friends would succeed as they went up to face the master werewolf.

I thought I heard something near the front door so I quickly ran past the staircase and out onto the back patio.

The patio actually led to an outdoor courtyard. The palace was so large that it completely surrounded the courtyard, making it feel like a private garden in the middle of towering architecture. Perhaps this would be a nice place under different circumstances (and a different time of the day).

Unlike the outside of the palace, the inner sanctuary of the courtyard was brightly lit. My eyes were immediately drawn to a ten-foot obelisk rising from the center of the courtyard.

My blood ran cold – it was the picture I had seen in the passageway – the one near the reptilian creatures. It seemed to glow green. *Your mind is playing tricks on you, isn't it?*

I had to see. As I approached the granite structure, it was smooth, and looking closely at it, I could see triangular markings just like in the tunnel of doom from which I had so narrowly escaped. *God no, everything in the passageway was real! The monsters are real!*

I felt like I was losing it. I knew that I was on the verge of a panic attack. *Keep it together,* I told myself as I backed away. That's when I turned and saw him.

CHAPTER 20

Augustine stood before me as a man, but his wolf was just below the surface. His eyes glowed and he smiled a menacing grin that hinted of very sharp teeth.

"You were with her," he said in a deep voice that seemed to echo in the walls of the palace's courtyard. "Yes, Nyarlothotep told me of you. He showed me everything in a vision."

"I don't have any business with you," I said, fear resonating in my voice. "I only seek Katherine's release."

"You may not think you have any business with me, but I have business with you," Augustine replied.

Even from his stance across the yard, I could tell his shoulders were changing. The wolf was coming soon.

"If you think I could let you or Katherine live, you are mistaken," Augustine challenged. "You two both know my identity and before long, all of the werewolves will be searching for me."

"It looks like you've made some enemies over the years," I taunted.

Augustine let out a howl so loud that it brought shivers to my spine.

Suddenly I felt a change in me starting to occur. *Shit no,* I thought, *Augustine is invoking me to become a werewolf so that he can fight me as a wolf!* No matter what, I could not let that happen. I was too new and there was a good possibility that Augustine would use the time it took me to change to attack and kill me.

I took a mad run toward him as he stood across the courtyard. Incredible pain shot through the tips of my fingers as I realized that sharp claws were growing where my human fingernails had been. The razor-like nails were growing so quickly that blood poured from my cuticles.

As I got within striking distance, I could see Augustine had changed as well. He was a wolf standing upright. That very moment, he was the spitting image of the fresco I had seen in the Temple of the Moon.

He was quick and ready to deflect my blow. With all my might, I lunged for his neck, grabbing onto fur and whatever I could as he threw me off with one swift motion of his hand. I flew through the air and landed hard on the ground.

"Fool!" Augustine shouted. "Do you think you can simply grab my neck?" There was such evil, such malice in his voice. Only one of us would be walking out of the palace tonight.

A thick layer of hair/fur pushed its way through my skin, causing my entire body to feel like I had a sudden extreme case of poison ivy and third-degree burns. I screamed. As my muscles contracted and my bones began to shift within their joints, I looked down at my hand and saw the one advantage I now had over Augustine – I had successfully removed the necklace from his neck. If my hunch was right, this might give me an edge I didn't have before.

I breathed loudly and heard myself let out a howl. I was changing. I moved quickly to position myself between the obelisk and Augustine, hoping to buy a few more seconds. As I did, I had another thought: *If the amulet makes him unstoppable, what if I wore it?* Not knowing if it would or

156

not, I had only one chance to put it on before my hands would no longer let me.

The necklace itself had broken when I pulled it off Augustine's neck, but I quickly made a knot to bind the two broken ends. I slipped it on over my neck just as Augustine made it around the obelisk.

As he pounced, I jumped up to avoid his strike. I thought I'd only jump a few feet, but to my surprise, I hurled myself into the air like some kind of superhero and landed on top of the obelisk!

Augustine let out a howl and jumped up to reach me. As he did, I jumped down on top of him and we collided in midair. With all my might, I slammed my paw into his chest and felt it push deep into his body cavity. We both fell to the earth with incredible force.

I heard the loud, unmistakable sound of breaking bones and thought for certain it was my arm, which was still inside of Augustine. Looking around, I saw that Augustine's skull had crushed on the pavement and he laid there, motionless.

We both stayed in that position for a few moments. Suddenly, Augustine's wolf form began to revert back to a man's. The cement behind his head was crimson with blood and there was more blood flowing from the open cavity in his chest area.

Reluctantly, I pulled my arm out of the gore and stood up. I realized that I could not *stand* upright as a bipedal human because I was already standing as a four-legged werewolf. I paced around Augustine's dead body and growled, not knowing if he would come back to life or not.

I then let out a loud howl and for the first time, realized that the howl echoing through the courtyard now carried the same menacing voice that once belonged to Augustine!

Strangely though, I could think clearly and was very much aware of my whereabouts and who I was. This was in stark contrast to the time I "sleepwalked" when I first came back to West Virginia and I did not know if the change occurred or not. It definitely had this time, and it wasn't yet a full moon.

The earth began to tremble and the obelisk began to glow a faint green. Matching the obelisk, the amulet also started glowing.

The obelisk's light grew stronger until it was shining so brightly that you could no longer see it as an obelisk but rather as a pillar of light. From within the light, a dark imposing figure stood. I had little doubt who it was.

"Nyarlothotep," I said.

"It seems I underestimated you," he replied, stepping out of the obelisk and into the courtyard.

"I thought you couldn't come here!" I said with utmost astonishment. It seems I could now talk. I was changing back. A wave of fatigue and nausea washed over me as I found myself naked and standing before the deity. I felt like I was going to puke, faint, or maybe both.

"I guess you were wrong," Nyarlothotep said. "You have been most amusing."

At that point, I thought he was going to do some kind of spell or something and kill me. I was too weak to fight him. However, what he said next surprised me.

"Because you have defeated Augustine, you now possess the Amulet of Lycan. Thus, I will give you a choice."

I looked up suspiciously but said nothing. Nyarlothotep continued, "You can assume Augustine's powers and the werewolf legacy will be yours, as it was his, to rule the wolf-kind and create more."

He paused and looked at me. Even then, I still could not see his face. "Or, you can give me the amulet right now and end the existences of werewolves forever."

As he spoke those words, he began to back up to the obelisk. Once again, it glowed brilliant green. He began to disappear.

I did not have to think about this. Nyarlothotep was getting the amulet back! I ran to him with all my might and grabbed the object clinging to my neck. I tried to throw it at him but it snagged on my neck and I stumbled forward into the obelisk.

Nyarlothotep had disappeared and I crashed into the obelisk. It was solid granite once more. With my head pressed against the cold stone, I could hear faint echoes of some forgotten chant coming from the rock. *Spirits of the deep, who never sleep, be kind to me.*

My mind was spinning. I had beaten the wolf, but ultimately failed to free mankind from the curse. I slumped onto the ground and cried. My nude body felt the first drop of rain as I knelt down in the courtyard.

CHAPTER 21

I don't know how long I had been there before Rudolfo and Max arrived. It may have been only minutes or maybe it was hours. The rain was pouring down and I made no move to retrieve my ripped clothes or move from my spot at the base of the obelisk.

"Get up," Max said kindly, helping me to my feet.

"Good job," Rudolfo said. "I welcome you to my pack any day. You singlehandedly defeated Augustine de Marnac!"

I took a glance at the corpse that lay only a few feet away. It too was soaking in the rain. The master werewolf was no more.

"Friend," Rudolfo said. "Let's find you some clothes in the palace. We still have some unfinished business to attend to."

"Rudolfo is right," Max replied. "We'll get you dried up then we are off to visit Zinoviy."

Max led me up to one of the rooms in the palace and helped me find a change of clothing. I was still dazed and confused about what just transpired.

How I longed for a night of lovemaking with Katherine at that moment. Her comfort and tending skills were most needed. I felt myself trembling but pushed on.

Max and Rudolfo were waiting by the Pombron. Rudolfo had not moved it from where he parked it and the front driver side wheel was still over the gunman. I grimaced as I glanced at him.

"He can't be helped now," Rudolfo said. "Hop in." He opened the back door and let me get inside.

Max was riding shotgun. He turned to me and said, "Rudolfo has notified Russian government officials of a modified version of what happened in the palace. They are working on a cover story to tie Augustine in with all sorts of illegal activity and this will look like a gang-related incident."

I simply nodded. At least they were working out the details. "What about Zinoviy?"

Rudolfo answered that one, "Once we find him, we will convince him to cooperate with Russian authorities, who will pass this data on to Interpol, and hopefully we can secure the princess's release."

"And if he doesn't cooperate?" I asked.

"Then Zinoviy dies." Rudolfo said matter-of-factly. I was convinced right then and there that Rudolfo was a sociopath and fortunately for us he was on our side. This man was a killing machine, not too unlike Augustine de Marnac. I slumped in the backseat and dozed as we left the palace grounds.

I didn't know how long we had been driving, but when I woke up the morning sun was shining and we were parked outside a small seaside eatery.

"Wake up Sleeping Beauty," Rudolfo said good-naturedly. I smiled.

A blond-haired waitress took our order and I left Rudolfo to give the order for all of us. I don't think I'll ever be able to learn to speak Russian and I definitely wasn't going to try this morning.

Warm food was brought to our table and a few minutes later, a man I assumed was the cook came by the table.

To my surprise, the cook immediately recognized Rudolfo and the two greeted each other like they were good friends. The two men exchanged some words in Russian and before long, the 'cook' had a look of worry in his eyes.

Rudolfo spoke in English for my benefit, "Zinoviy here wants to speak to us in the kitchen."

The cook is Zinoviy? That didn't make sense.

As we made it to the kitchen, I realized that it was no ordinary kitchen. Sure, there was a kitchen but behind one of the preparation areas was a door that looked like it was part of the tiled wall. The cook opened up this hidden door and we all walked inside. He closed it quickly.

Rudolfo produced the empty casings for Zinoviy's inspection and the man did not deny making the bullets. Zinoviy seemed to be greatly concerned that his former employer would come after if he revealed who his employer was.

Rudolfo advised Zinoviy that Augustine was no longer a threat and when Zinoviy still didn't believe him, Rudolfo reached for my shirt and pulled at the collar.

I was briefly stunned by this sudden movement and was unsure what he was doing. Zinoviy's eyes got very big when he saw the amulet hanging around my neck.

Before long, he pulled out a notebook he had in his desk containing careful records of all the rounds of ammunition that he ever had made for Augustine and agreed to speak with the authorities about the matter.

He telephoned an individual who I assumed was an investigator and directed the person to go to the palace to investigate a mafia-related crime and could provide key details regarding Augustine's involvement in the framing of Katherine.

After the investigator was done at the palace, he met Rudolfo down in Agriya, where Zinoviy gave his statement and worked on a special plea bargain. I imagined he would be getting off light, but my only hope was that this effort would be enough to convince Spanish authorities to let Katherine go.

Shortly thereafter, Max was on the telephone with Julian and relayed the information we had uncovered. It took another two days to clear things up in Agirya and before long we were back on the Leer, this time heading for Madrid.

When the jet touched down, Max and I took a taxi to the jail to meet with Katherine.

After about a half-hour of paperwork and long conversations with Spanish authorities, Max was able to get us in to see her. As I looked at her, my heart melted. She really was the woman I truly loved, my wolf, and my mate.

She gave me a hug and we shared a passionate kiss. She pulled the necklace off and looked carefully at it.

"It's hard to believe the son of a bitch is dead. Truly dead," she said. I simply nodded. Her hands trembled as she handed the necklace back to me.

"Thank you so much," she added.

"You're welcome," I whispered in her ear.

It took another week, but Katherine was eventually released. The Russians produced enough evidence to link Augustine de Marnac with the murders in Madrid and this seemed to satisfy them that Katherine was innocent.

She got out just in time, as the next full moon was only a week away.

Back at her flat when we were alone she told me, "We have to finish what we started."

"And that is?" I played dumb.

"We have to finish the mating ritual," she replied. "That must happen during the full moon."

"I'm up for it; whatever it is."

She grinned and we kissed.

One week later, we were out at the pack farm in Escopete. Max and some of the other Madrid werewolves were in attendance.

A large bonfire was set up and for the most part, it was as if we were all having a normal get-together. Perhaps we were.

As the full moon rose up we all began to change. Katherine and I turned in unison and took off into the woods.

ABOUT THE AUTHOR

Gary Lee Vincent is an accomplished author, musician, and entrepreneur. In 2009, he founded Burning Bulb Publishing to help promote up-and-coming authors.

In 2010, his horror novel *Darkened Hills* was selected as Book of the Year Winner by *ForeWord Reviews Magazine* and became the pilot novel for **DARKENED – THE WEST VIRGINIA VAMPIRE SERIES**, which includes the follow-up books *Darkened Hollows*, *Darkened Waters*, and *Darkened Souls*. More information on this series can be found at **www.DarkenedHills.com.**

Gary was a contributing editor on *The Big Book of Bizarro*, *Westward Hoes* and *Rise of the Dead* anthologies. He is also the creator of *The Tailsman* comic book based on the story of the same name in *Westward Hoes* and is working on a second comic from the anthology titled *Demoneye*.

Gary's official website is **www.GaryVincent.com.**

GARY LEE VINCENT'S
DARKENED
THE WEST VIRGINIA VAMPIRE SERIES

DARKENED HILLS

When evil descends on a small West Virginia town, who will survive?

Jonathan did not start out his life to become a rambler, it just worked out that way. William was a troubled youth with something to hide. Both were from Melas, a small town tucked away in the West Virginia hills... a town where disappearances are happening more and more frequently.

After the suicide of a wanted serial killer, the townsfolk thought the nightmare was over. But when a centuries-old vampire is discovered they find out the hard way it's just getting started. Dark secrets can only stay hidden for so long and when the devil comes to collect, there will be hell to pay. Can Jonathan and William find a way to stop the vampire before it's too late? Find out in *Darkened Hills!*

DARKENED HOLLOWS

In the heart-stopping sequel to the award-winning *Darkened Hills*, Jonathan and William must return to West Virginia to face possible criminal charges stemming from their last visit to the damned town of Melas, where both had narrowly escaped the clutches of a vampire seethe.

And as livestock start mysteriously getting murdered with all of their blood drained, worried farmers are searching for answers - leaving the local Sheriff and his deputy racing against time to learn the cause before a more violent crime is committed.

Burning Bulb
PUBLISHING

WWW.DARKENEDHILLS.COM

GARY LEE VINCENT'S
DARKENED
THE WEST VIRGINIA VAMPIRE SERIES

DARKENED WATERS

When the world goes to hell, the chosen must arise!

As Talman Cane orchestrates a flood of epic proportions in this third installment of the *Darkened* series the towns of Melas and Tarklin are caught completely off guard by the deluge. Hell-bent on finishing what they started, the evil brothers return to the lunatic asylum to take care of the witnesses and add to the ever-growing army of the undead.

Aided by Lucifer himself and the insane vampire demon Legion, the stage is set to channel all of the forces of hell to come forth. In an all-out race to survive, Jonathan, William, and Amanda soon discover they are up against impossible odds as Lucifer opens the Gateway to Hell, ushering in the zombie apocalypse and the End Times.

DARKENED SOULS

Melas and the Madison House are about to be rebuilt.
True evil is about to be reborne!

Young ex-priest and vampire-killer William is drawn back to the West Virginian town that almost killed him, where his vampire arch-enemy Victor Rothenstein still stalks the earth.

The town of Melas lies destroyed after the battle of the End of Days. But why is wealthy Jackie Nixon so eager to rebuild it using the bone dust of murdered souls?

Terrible evil has visited before, but the Gateway to Hell is about to be reopened in a horrific climax. And this time – it's personal.

WWW.DARKENEDHILLS.COM

Burning Bulb
PUBLISHING

THE TAILSMAN

From the creators of *The Big Book of Bizarro* and *Westward Hoes* comes a new comic unlike anything you have ever seen!

He's hot on the trail, looking for some *tail...*

Sly Franko was a man of the West, a forger of the wild frontier. Like the Country Western song that would be written years after he died, the words, "Faster horses, younger women, and more money," seemed to be the anthem of this horn dog cowboy.

Franko would ride into town on a blazing saddle, find the closest saloon to wet the whistle, belly up to a good card game, and find him a hot-loving hussy to get his cowpoke on with.

However, Sly might have met his match when a visit to bathroom leads to terror and death. Can Sly and his poker buddies solve the mystery before more of the townsfolk are murdered? Find out in this exciting premier issue of *The Tailsman!*

WWW.BURNINGBULBCOMICS.COM

OTHER GREAT TITLES FROM

Burning Bulb

PUBLISHING

WWW.BURNINGBULBPUBLISHING.COM

ANTHOLOGIES
BIZARRO AND TRANSGRESSIVE FICTION

THE BIG BOOK OF BIZARRO

The Big Book of Bizarro brings together the peculiar prose of an international cast of the most grotesquely-gonzo, genre-grinding modern writers who ever put pen to paper (or mouse to pad), including:

NIGHT OF THE LIVING DEAD horror writers John Russo & George Kosana; HUSTLER MAGAZINE erotica contributors Eva Hore, Andrée Lachapelle, & J. Troy Seate and established Bizarro genre authors D. Harlan Wilson, William Pauley III, Wol-vriey, Laird Long, Richard Godwin and so many more!

From Alien abductions to Zombie sex, The Big Book of Bizarro contains OVER FIFTY STORIES of the most outrélandish transgressive fiction that you'll ever lay your capricious and curious hands upon!

WARNING: This book may be one of the most controversial and dangerous books you'll ever read.

WESTWARD HOES

Nine outlaw writers rode into town from obscurity to pen nine tantalizing tales of horror and fantasy, and leaving once they branded their own personal marks on the weird western genre and became living legends of the American Frontier experience.

Like drunken Indian scouts, the writers fervidly tracked down and captured the Western genre, tore off its fashionable veneer and ravished its exposed essence.

So belly up to the bar with your favorite soiled dove and enjoy perusing these thrilling tales of Old West debauchery, danger and desire; compiled by the publisher of The Big Book of Bizarro and featuring the bizarro novella *Big Trouble in Little Ass* by Wol-vriey.

Burning Bulb
PUBLISHING

ANTHOLOGIES
BIZARRO AND TRANSGRESSIVE FICTION

THE BIG BOOK OF BIZARRO SPECIAL KINDLE EDITIONS

OTHER AWESOME COLLECTIONS

RISE OF THE DEAD

AN EARTH-SHATTERING ANTHOLOGY OF ZOMBIE TERROR

Featuring Stories By:

John A. Russo   Tyson Blue   E.L. Stice   Nelson W. Pyles

Andy Rausch   Stephen Spignesi   R.D. Riley   Zakary McGaha

David J. Fairhead   Gary Lee Vincent   David C. Hayes   Rachel Montgomery

Paul Victor Wargelin   David F. Walker   William Vitka

Rich Bottles Jr.   Douglas Brode

RISE OF THE DEAD - a collection of seventeen tales of unspeakable zombie terror. Featuring a foreword and short story by John A. Russo!

www.TheJohnRusso.com

Burning Bulb
PUBLISHING

NIGHT OF THE LIVING DEAD

Why does **Night of the Living Dead** hit with such chilling impact?
Is it because everyday people in a commonplace house are suddenly the
victims of a monstrous invasion? Or is it because the ghouls who surround
the house with grasping claws were once ordinary people, too?

Decide for yourself as you read, and the horror grips you. All the
cannibalism, suspense and frenzy of the smash-hit move are here in the
novel.

www.TheJohnRusso.com

Burning Bulb
PUBLISHING

WEST VIRGINIA-THEMED HUMORROROTICA

BY RICH BOTTLES JR.

HELLHOLE WEST VIRGINIA

From the heights of Mothman's perch high atop the Silver Bridge in Point Pleasant to the depths of Hellhole Cavern in Pendleton County, evil lurks within the shadows as the sun sets upon the haunted hills and hollows of West Virginia.

Bizarro author Rich Bottles Jr. blows the coffin lid off horror genre clichés with this tour de force cast of Eco-friendly vampires, beach-yearning zombies and sex-starved she-devils.

LUMBERJACKED

If you are easily offended or do not possess a truly depraved sense of humor, this story may not be the light summer reading fare you desire. As for the four feisty female freshmen stranded on top of West Virginia's third highest mountain, they have no choice but to experience the sick, twisted debauchery and perverted mayhem described deep inside the tight unbroken bindings of this horrific missive.

Lumberjacked takes the reader to a nightmarish world where character development and aesthetic integrity are prematurely cut short by the swinging axes of maniacal lumberjacks, who are hell bent on death and destruction in the remote forests of Appalachia. And at the climax, when paranoia crosses over to the paranormal, Lumberjacked makes Deliverance look like a family raft trip down the Lower Gauley.

THE MANACLED

What happens when twin brothers lease out the former West Virginia State Penitentiary with the false purpose of filming a documentary on supernatural phenomena, but their true intention is to make a pornographic movie?

Chaos ensues as the disturbed spirits of murdered convicts, along with the reanimated dead from the neighboring Indian Burial Mound, take their vengeance on the unwary and undressed trespassers.

Zombies, ghosts, mobsters and porn collide in this bizarro tale from horror author Rich Bottles Jr.

Burning Bulb
PUBLISHING

DETOUR TO ARMAGEDDON BY SOLON TSANGARAS

"An all-pervasive breakout of ghoulish pandemonium related
with unbridled glee and terror."
—John Russo, author of *Night of the Living Dead*

WHO WILL SURVIVE? WILL THEY WANT TO?

Enter a world where your best friend, your neighbor, your mother
or father, just aren't the same people you knew. But THEY aren't the
real enemy...

Join groups of survivors as they make their way across this
once-great nation that has been devastated by a man-made plague
created by corporate greed and fed by self-serving men who are
hungry for power and control.

Burning Bulb
PUBLISHING

WOL-VRIEY
BIZARRO AND TRANSGRESSIVE FICTION

BOSTON POSH

In 2028 AD, the USA is a nation ravaged by hungry dragons and dinosaurs. In Boston, Massachusetts, private eye Bud Malone is hired to rescue a kidnapped heiress. But nothing is as it seems.

Malone works to unravel a tangled web involving Boston Chinatown, a 200-year-old woman with a 9-year-old body, white robots, a human-liver-eating psychopath, a golem, a porcelain dragon, and a snake goddess with a crush on him. There's also a woman obsessed with chicken sex. Then Malone meets Posh Lane, a gorgeous call girl who's desperate to quit her pimp.

Romantic sparks ignite between Posh and Malone, but Posh's past suddenly catches up with her in a BIG way. To save Posh, Malone agrees to run a quest for Earth's new rulers, the Forks. But, Malone has no idea that agreeing to the Fork's odd request will send him on the weirdest trip he's ever been on in his life.

VAGINA MUNDI

Rachel Risk is a professional thief with super-strong hair that can stretch like tentacles to manipulate objects. Ashley Status has both a digitally augmented brain, and 'muscle-purses' in her arms and legs in which she stores inflatable objects—cars, guns, rocket launchers, etc.

When Raye is framed as the fall girl in a jewel robbery, the pair flee Chicago's vengeful robot gangsters and take refuge in the Hotel Bizarre, where the gorgeous 'vagina singer,' Femina, is performing for a week.

But the Hotel Bizarre is even stranger than its name suggests, and very soon Raye and Ash are involved in an deadly adventure, a struggle for survival the likes of which they'd never imagined possible—with loads of deviant sex, drugs, music, and violence at every turn. And just what is the old woman in the skin desert really doing with all those cats glued to her walls?

Vagina Mundi—a Bizarro Hymn in praise of WOMAN!

Burning Bulb
PUBLISHING

WOL-VRIEY
BIZARRO AND TRANSGRESSIVE FICTION

VEGAN VAMPIRE VAGINAS

The biggest bank heist in US history. And Tom Palmer can't remember pulling it off. And no, this isn't your standard case of amnesia. After a one-night-stand gone horribly wrong, Boston salesman Tom Palmer wakes up with a vagina implanted in his left hand. Then his day gets worse.

Tom is transported across space-time to a nightmare version of Boston, one where the Bizarro virus has transformed half the population into cannibals. Worst of all, Tom discovers that in this new Boston, he's the infamous gangster Pussypalm, wanted for robbing the Federal Reserve Bank of Boston a year ago. He also learns that the vagina in his hand is prophetic, i.e. it talks . . . after sex.

With 130 people left dead during his bank heist and six billion dollars missing, Tom knows he's living on borrowed time. It is in his best interests not to remember anything. Because once he does . . .

VEGAN ZOMBIE APOCALYPSE

In the post-apocalypse worlderness, zombies rule the earth. They're allergic to meat, and brains literally make them explode. Zombies now eat blood potatoes, parasitic tubers grown in the flesh of humancows corralled in maximum security farms. Two fugitives meet in the ancient ruins of Texas. The first is Soil 15-f, a womancow who's escaped her farm a week before she's due to be killed and her blood potato crop harvested. The second fugitive is Able Kane, former head necros food technician, now sentenced to death for heresy. But Soil is no ordinary humancow.

Unknown to herself, she's the vegan zombie agricultural revolution, and the zombies desperately want her back. And the necros equally desperately want Able Kane dead. He's fled with a forbidden discovery which will reshape the world for the worse if used. And Able is just hardheaded/misguided enough to use it.

Burning Bulb
PUBLISHING

THE FALL OF TOMORROW

Hopelessness... How do you protect your loved ones when Hell itself opens its insidious mouth?
Horror... Nightmarish Creatures invade your world and there is nowhere to hide.
Blood... How long can you hold out before they come for you?
Pain... Where do you run to avoid being eaten alive by monsters with a voracious appetite for your flesh?
Screams... While you selfishly run for your own life.
Questions... Who is to blame? Where did they come from? How many people survived...and how does the human race find the means to fight back?

THE FALL OF TOMORROW is man's last tale of desperation told by those that are striving to salvage some hope against a ravenous bastion of evil beasts bent on ruling our world.

"David Fairhead writes compelling stories that offer very human characters and very inhuman monsters. There is no subtlety in Fairhead's imagination - he is simply dying to scare the hell out of you."
    - Nelson W Pyles - author of DEMONS, DOLLS AND MILKSHAKES

Burning Bulb
PUBLISHING

BLOODLETTING: A TALE OF REVENGE BY ANDY RAUSCH

"Relentless... Addictive... The kind of nightmare you don't want to wake up from."
—Heywood Gould, screenwriter of *Rolling Thunder*

He was just an average Joe. But when he finds his family held at gunpoint by merciless thugs, he's told he must murder a Mafia chieftain if he ever wishes to see his loved ones again.

Against all odds, Joe keeps his end of the bargain, but the criminals don't. Now at his wits end, Joe is pushed beyond his breaking point and forced to exact bloody revenge against those who've done him and his family wrong in this powerful and violent novella by author Andy Rausch (*Mad World*).

"Andy Rausch has a tight noir style that combines gritty, realistic drama with a cinematic flair that makes for a powerful, compelling (somewhat Stephen Kingesque), authentically visual reading experience."
—Stephen Spignesi, author of *Dialogues*

Burning Bulb
PUBLISHING

MAD WORLD BY ANDY RAUSCH

"*Mad World* is dark, twisted, no-holds-barred fun."
—Jason Starr, author of *Bust*, *Slide*, and *The Max*

EVERYONE'S PLAYING AN ANGLE IN THE CITY OF ANGELS

Mad World tells the stories of a black hitman who doubles as a university professor, a Catholic priest who longs to be a gangster, a would-be author from Kansas, a gay phone sex operator who claims he's straight, a group of rich twentysomethings playing a deadly game of life and death, a vicious Mafia boss, and a sleazy Hollywood movie director. As each of their stories intersect, the body count piles up and the action comes nonstop in this tense, white-knuckle thriller by first-time author Andy Rausch.

"A wild ride. If you like it gangster, *Mad World* delivers."
—Daniel Birch, author of *Get Some*

Burning Bulb
PUBLISHING

ELVIS PRESLEY, CIA ASSASSIN BY ANDY RAUSCH

"I can guarantee you. Read this book and you'll never look at Elvis the same way again!"
~ Douglas Brode, author of ELVIS CINEMA AND POPULAR CULTURE

SOON TO BE A MAJOR MOTION PICTURE

In 1970, singer Elvis Presley secretly met with President Richard Nixon. This new comedic novel imagines that Presley became a Central Intelligence Agency operative, eventually moving up through the ranks to become a skilled assassin.

Presented in an oral history fashion, the book tells us about Presley's secret transformation by the people who knew him best.

Did he fake his death in 1977? Was Presley involved with the Watergate scandal? The Iran hostage crisis? Communicating with aliens?

Read this book to find out the answers to these and many more questions.

Burning Bulb
PUBLISHING

"A sense of infectious fun, straight from the author's pen."
— Nightmare Library

From Legendary Horror Writer
JOHN A. RUSSO

LIVING THINGS

"Russo carries his talent for the horrific neatly over into the novel form."
— West Coast Review of Books

LIVING THINGS

Beneath the shimmering Miami sun sprawls one of the Mafia's biggest empires, a glittering world of lavish beachfront mansions, neon-painted nightclubs, beautiful women, expensive cars—and absolute control over the state's billion-dollar drug trade. But, one by one, its ganglords and henchmen are falling prey to a new rival. His powers are fueled by monstrous ancient rituals; his hellish undead legions slaughter mobsters and innocent citizens alike, his unholy lust for power is virtually unstoppable.

Now a burned-out ex-detective and a brilliant anthropologist must enter a gruesome, nightmare world to fight this master of malevolence and illusion. Their time is short, their weapons few, and they face an ultimate, terrifying choice - annihilation or the loss of their souls to the eternal torment of those who never die. . .

www.TheJohnRusso.com

Burning Bulb
PUBLISHING

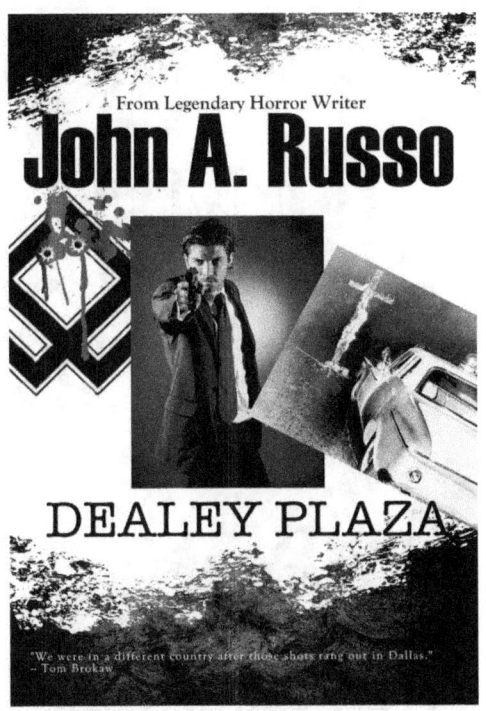

DEALEY PLAZA

From legendary horror and suspense writer JOHN RUSSO comes a
harrowing tale where no one is safe!

Dealey Plaza is one of the most notorious places in America, and
when youthful conspiracy buffs go there in 1964 to stage their own
reenactment of the Kennedy Assassination, four of them are
brutally murdered ~ the first victims of a hate-filled legacy that
continues for four more decades.

The survivors of that long-ago Dallas trip, each of them now icons
of the American way of life, are about to be honored ~ or killed.

Who will live and who will die? Will it be country-western star Lori
McCoy? Her loving husband? Her scheming ex-husband? Or the
case-hardened FBI agent and longtime friend who risks his life
trying to protect them?

www.DealeyPlazaBook.com

Burning Bulb
PUBLISHING

LIMB TO LIMB

SUCH A PRETTY GIRL . . .
Tiffany Blake was a beautiful long-limbed dancer with a glorious future and the backing of a rich benefactor. Then a monstrous accident severed her leg at the hip.

SUCH A COLD, CRUEL KNIFE . . .
And now her fellow dancers are disappearing without a trace. One by one they fall victim to a dark and deadly pattern of evil – caught by the bloody, brutal logic that would have them pay with their lovely bodies for the cruel fate of another . . .victims of the sadistic madman whose flashing knife will make them writhe a gruesome new dance.

www.TheJohnRusso.com

Burning Bulb
PUBLISHING

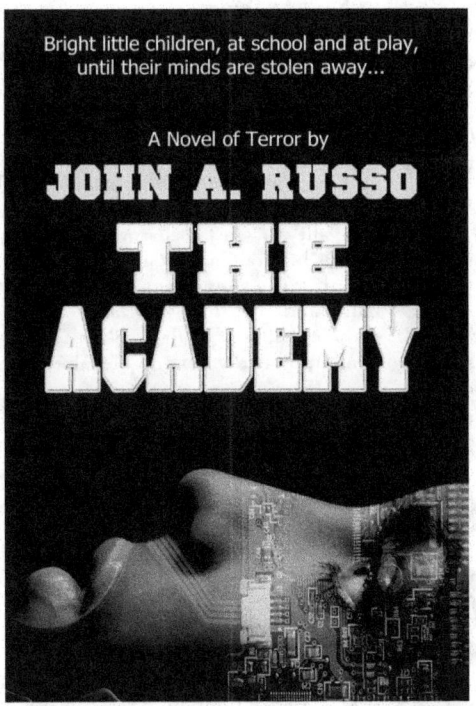

Bright little children, at school and at play,
until their minds are stolen away...

A Novel of Terror by

JOHN A. RUSSO

THE ACADEMY

THE ACADEMY

The Academy. It's every parent's dream, turning their little darlings into geniuses, superachievers, perfect little children.

And if there's a problem, the Academy fixes that too. It's a simple operation. Just a little device. Then a teeny pink scar on a tender little skull . . .

One boy knows the secret. Now he wants his mind back. But it's much, much too late. Too late for anything but the ugly feelings. The bad feelings. The messy sexy feelings. The knife-cold hatred, the murderous rage, for total, screaming, blood-drenching revenge . . .

www.TheJohnRusso.com

Burning Bulb
PUBLISHING

THE HAGS OF BLACK COUNTY

by Michelle Bowser

Ruled by a committee of Hags, and fueled by toothless rivalries, Black County lurks just far enough out of the way to be completely unnoticed by the rest of civilization. Its inhabitants have been mentally warped for generations and the land itself seems to have the power to drive anyone unlucky enough to visit into ridiculous hillbilly madness. When a construction Company needs to bury a pipeline through its ludicrous hills and valleys, a twisted charm goes to work and every aspect of already bizarre Black County life takes a gory turn for the hysterical. Take a preposterous trip along with its citizens, both native and new, through escapades such as the Hag parade, the grand opening of Madame Skunk's House of Ill Repute, the demolition derby riot and the rabid, zombie clown apocalypse.

THE ABANDONED SOUL

by Daniel Sellers

After spending most of his 20s in a drug and alcohol fueled daze, a young man finally hits rock bottom. Having used up his friends and their good graces, he ends up squatting in an abandoned house. Forcibly sobering he begins to realize that he is not alone in this abandoned house. Left with one last friend and a mountain of regrets, he must decide if this presence is a guilty conscience, or a malicious hunter.

WE WISH YOU A HAPPY KILLDAY

by Jason Heroux

"We Wish You a Happy Killday" is the story of an international b eloved holiday called "Killday" where one day a year everyone over the age of fifteen is permitted to register for a license allowing them to kill one other person. But this year Chad Ovenstock doesn't feel like killing anyone. His friends and family urge him to participate in the festivities, but he can't seem to get into the holiday spirit. On the day before Killday Chad comes in contact with Ambrose, an old friend who suffered a nervous breakdown and is now part of The One Ant Army, a mysterious cult dedicated to making the future disappear. When the holiday finally arrives Chad refuses to participate and tries to survive on his own, surrounded by constant gunfire, countless corpses, and the nagging suspicion that Ambrose may have secretly brainwashed him into becoming a member of The One Ant Army cult.

Burning Bulb
PUBLISHING

www.ingramcontent.com/pod-product-compliance
Lightning Source LLC
Chambersburg PA
CBHW071234130626
46556CB00003B/999